WHAT YOU NEED

WHAT YOU NEED

ANDREW FORBES

Invisible Publishing

Halifax & Toronto

Library and Archives Canada Cataloguing in Publication

Forbes, Andrew, 1976-, author
     What you need / Andrew Forbes.

Short stories.
ISBN 978-1-926743-54-7 (pbk.)

     I. Title.

PS8611.O7213W43 2015   C813'.6   C2015-901244-9

Cover & Interior designed by Megan Fildes

Typeset in Laurentian and Slate by Megan Fildes
With thanks to type designer Rod McDonald

Printed and bound in Canada

Invisible Publishing
Halifax & Toronto
www.invisiblepublishing.com

We acknowledge the support of the Canada Council for the Arts, which last year
invested $157 million to bring the arts to Canadians throughout the country.

Invisible Publishing recognizes the support of the Province of Nova Scotia
through the Department of Communities, Culture & Heritage. We are pleased
to work in partnership with the Culture Division to develop and promote our
cultural resources for all Nova Scotians.

For my parents, for their
lifelong encouragement.

"These are the days of miracle and wonder. Don't cry, baby, don't cry, don't cry."

— Paul Simon

WHAT YOU NEED

From the driver's seat of my rental car I watch the landscape of my upbringing approach and recede at 85 miles an
hour. The fields in their robust spring colour, the blondness
of wheat, the green of new corn stalks, sunflowers ringing a
staid grey farmhouse. Home again, central Illinois.

On Route 51, ringing Decatur, I pull into a rest stop near
the Blue Mound turnoff, get out, stretch my legs. The air
is hot and close. I swallow an Aspirin, undo a button at my
collar. A bead of sweat rolls from my temple, along my jaw
and across to my chin before it slides down the front of my
throat. The sun slips down the sky.

James Goodspear, my older brother, used to go by Jamie.
Now most people call him Jim. I don't know when that happened exactly. But even Janet, his wife, started off calling
him Jamie and switched somewhere along the way. To his
students at Macon County High, where he teaches math, he
remains Mr. Goodspear, of course. Ms. Canty, the English
teacher, his girlfriend, calls him Jimbo. In this she is alone.

As I approach Blue Mound I stop at a grubby little gas
station and pick up some beer, as is expected of me. Once
I get to Jamie's the beer goes into the chest freezer in his
large, clean garage. When the kids go to bed Jamie and I will

climb a ladder and take the beer up on the roof of his house, the bungalow on a couple of acres that he and Janet bought the year they were married, when Jamie was 29 and Janet 24. It's a nice little house, a lot like the one he and I grew up in, and no more than 15 miles away from there.

I arrive at dusk this Friday ahead of the long weekend, pulling into the driveway to find Jamie and Janet in lawn chairs out front, their kids Angela and Robert splashing in a blue plastic wading pool. The gravel crunches and pops under my tires as I pull in, and the car begins to click after I shut it off. I step out into the warm air of the coming night, the paper bag in my hands containing a pair of six-packs. Robbie and Angela run toward me in their bright bathing suits, their delicate torsos heaving and a tangle of their wet limbs around my legs and waist. Jamie approaches and shakes my hand. Janet offers me a kiss on the cheek.

"Hello, Janet."

"How was the drive, Richie?" she asks.

"Flat," I say, and we both smile.

"Come on, you two," she says to the children, "time to get ready for bed."

"We said they could stay up until you got here," Jamie says, taking the paper bag from my hands and heading toward the garage.

We climb up onto the roof just as we would do when we were kids, and we watch the last of the light drain from the west, looking out over the sky and the dimming fields. Over the drone of crickets, we hear Janet inside the house talking to the dog in her ex-smoker's rasp. Up here we can see the railroad tracks, their course a slash across the landscape, heading off toward Decatur to the northeast and St. Louis to the southwest in a line that suggests efficiency, and a hundred forgotten towns like Blue Mound along the way.

As the stars appear over our heads I imagine them making a sound like beer can pull-tabs, *crack-pop-fizz*. I recline, feel the roughness of the shingles on my elbows and lower back.

"Memorial Day," Jamie says. "About goddamn time, isn't it?"

"Thought it would never get here," I say.

"Might as well be Labor Day for your Cubs," he says. "Season's over."

"That's fucking rich coming from a Royals fan," I tell him, then swallow a mouthful of beer.

"How's the big city treating my little brother?"

"Cruelly."

"What about those big city women?"

"Even more cruelly," I deadpan.

"Plenty of room around here for a guy to settle down, you know. Lots of good women waiting to marry."

"You should know. You got two of 'em."

"Careful there," he says, then chuckles. "I know, you got the city in your head now, probably never leave. But you won't see a sky like that in Chicago," he says, nodding toward the pink and orange horizon. I look at his face, softly lit by the dead sun. He's earnest, I'll say that for him, and deeply in love with this place, despite the headaches he's created here.

"You've got me there," I say.

I get through four Buds by the time Jamie drains the last of his six, and then we lie on our backs for a while, feeling the earth spinning below us.

"Glad you came," Jamie says to me just before we make our wobbly way back down the ladder.

Inside, it smells of spaghetti and meatballs and a time-worn dampness. Jamie points to my spot on the sofa, set up for me just like it always is. "You need anything?" he asks. I shake my head no. Then he heads down the hall on tiptoes, past the kids' rooms, before slipping into bed next to a slumbering Janet.

I wake up to eggs frying and coffee percolating in the Mr. Coffee machine, and the house already feels hot. Standing at the range with her back to me is Janet, wearing a short robe, her dark brown hair like an angry bird's nest. Hazel-eyed Janet Evans is sturdily beautiful now, just as she was in high school. She has wide shoulders like a swimmer, long arms, August-brown skin even in deepest January. She has nicks and scars covering those parts of her body left exposed by shorts and tank tops because she has spent her life with men who took her at her word that she was willing to do whatever heavy work was at hand. Her father had her driving a tractor by the time she hit 11. With Jamie she has lived with her hands, laying sod, swinging careless hammers into her thumb, scraping her knees in the jagged gravel of the driveway while kneeling to check for the source of the oil leaking from their dusty Suburban. I visited them five years ago in the middle of a hot and dry July, and even eight months pregnant she'd be on the riding mower once a week, and afterwards humping the gas weed trimmer around the yard, wearing tall rubber boots and leather gloves, safety glasses and big orange muffs to protect her ears, the kind you see on baggage handlers. A couple of years later, pregnant with Robert, she spurred the labour on by hefting around packages of laminate flooring that Jamie was laying in the kitchen. The next morning she was in the hospital, and by lunchtime she was holding little Robbie.

What Jamie doesn't know is that Janet and I spent a night together when I was back from school for Thanksgiving during my junior year at Iowa. She and Jamie had gone out a couple of times, and he was pretty serious about her. I knew that. I was at a party. It poured rain that night. Janet was there and she looked so pretty. We split a six-pack of wine coolers after somebody stole my beer. She got a bit frisky, and I wasn't arguing.

She and I have never spoken of it since, and it's been so long that I honestly don't believe it's what either of us is actively thinking about when Jamie leaves the room for a minute. It's there, of course, hazy and indistinct, but real. But it no longer requires thought; it has become a part of who we are.

Jamie still counts himself a Royals fan, which probably means that were I to tell him of this he'd be capable of forgiving any of my transgressions with that oversized heart of his. But it would remain, I know, a nettlesome thing there between us, and so I will die withholding this truth from him: I want his wife more than any other woman I have ever known. I might even say that I fell in love with Janet that night. Might, if I knew just what that meant, what that felt like for people. I guess, since it is a thing I haven't felt since, with any other woman, that might be my clue. The women I have dated have all paled next to Janet. The underdressed Chicago girls on trains, or in bars, with their loaded glances and their earnest curiosity, do not rouse me once I have compared their dewy cheeks and scrubbed, tawny limbs to Janet's lived-in skin. I look at other women, of course, and date some of them, but to defeat any misapplied pangs of desire I have only to remember our one night together, when I was 19 and she a year younger, her soft shoulders and the simple manner in which she raised her hips to help me slide off her underwear. It is a dusty memory, but it has come to me more times than I can count, and I have worried it smooth like a stone.

The kids put ketchup on their eggs. Jamie puts it on his steak. Every Saturday morning Jamie has steak and eggs, a thing I thought only the English and the very rich did until I learned of my brother's weekly ritual. Janet offers to make me some, but I opt for Corn Flakes and a banana.

Today Jamie's wearing what I call his Republican recruiter's uniform. He really goes for the Dockers look, all khaki and sky blue, beige, and white, but truthfully it suits his lean frame and close-cropped head, perpetually buzzed to minimize the aging effect of his balding. We both got our father's wiry frame; so far only Jamie's been lucky enough to inherit Dad's hair loss. I'm dressed in black this day, as usual, and I'll probably appear conspicuous here in pickup country.

We climb into the minivan—it's got a DVD player with a small monitor that descends from the roof just behind the front seats, to keep the kids quiet on long trips—and as we roll down the country lanes he slips in a Led Zeppelin CD.

Like most American boys, we experienced a Zeppelin phase, spanning two or three summers. We grew our hair out and spent most of our time in the basement rec room, dark and musty and cluttered, sitting before Dad's Radio Shack turntable and boxy speakers, listening to *Led Zeppelin IV* and *Houses of the Holy*.

This is just what Jamie's trying to invoke by putting this on, this newly released live CD culled from thirty-year-old tapes, and turning it up until his Caravan's speakers are straining. He is calling on a time in the memory when we were teenagers, devious and grubby, curious and sullen.

And it works.

"Go faster," I tell him.

We're off to the Home Depot in Decatur, some twenty minutes away, to get lumber and supplies, because my brother and I don't know what to with each other when we're not drinking on the roof. So we build stuff. Truthfully, it is one of my favourite things, and not something I often have the opportunity to do back in Chicago, where I and my apartment-kept friends have janitors and superintendents and service people to tidy the edges and join the nuts and bolts of our daily existences. But when I visit Jamie he's careful to have a project to keep us busy. This Memorial Day weekend we're to rebuild his front porch, which was shoddily made to begin with and now stands rotting on pilings sent wandering off level by frost heave and the thousand bodies that have bounded over them.

As we rush along highways bracketed by cornfields, we begin to discuss our list of materials, giving me a chance to slip into a practical voice I don't get much chance to use in Chicago. We talk about two-by-fours and how best to hang stairs when Jamie suddenly turns to me and says, "Hey," and I can tell this will have nothing to do with lumber or fasteners, "okay if we make a quick stop?"

"Where at?"

"Friend's house."

"You're driving."

Brenda Canty is red-haired and freckly, short, round, and inviting. Even her eyelashes are a pale orange, and her smile takes up half her face. She's younger than Jamie, but not by much, I'd guess. I don't want to like her, but I do.

On this bright morning she's reading a paper at a round plastic table on the front stoop of her small townhouse just outside Decatur. She pops up when she sees Jimbo's van pull into the visitors' spaces across the row, and bounds over to greet him. There's a half a moment's hesitation in her step when I emerge from the passenger side, but my brother must shoot her an "it's okay" look, because she continues to advance right into his arms.

"Jimbo," she says, "and is this Richie?"

"The one and only," he answers, and she comes around the front of the van to shake my hand. "I'm Brenda," she says. "Happy to know you."

"Likewise, Brenda," I say. Jamie walks up behind her and joins his hands around her waist. She holds them and rocks gently side to side.

"Wow. You know, I feel like I know you," she says to me.

"Brenda, honey," Jamie says, "me and Richie're headed into the Home Depot, so I thought I'd take care of that patching job for you."

"Right. Oh, right. You know, that'd be such a big help to me, Jim." She turns to me. "Richie, your brother took down a bathroom cabinet for me. It was sort of in the way, you know? And he took it down off the wall, and wouldn't you know there's the ugliest hole back there?"

"Big hole punched right into the wall," he says, nodding to me. "I'm just gonna take another quick look at it," he calls, bounding up the step and through the screen door.

Brenda and I are left standing on the small front lawn. There is a silence. "What's new in the world?" I ask, pointing to her *USA Today.*

"What's ever new?" she says, and we both offer polite laughter.

There is a pause. "I understand you're a teacher?"

She says, "Oh, yes. I love it. That's how I know your brother. I guess he told you that."

"Yes, he did." We laugh.

"You know, I hope this isn't uncomfortable for you," she says. "I don't really know what to say here."

"No, I don't either."

Brenda Canty gives me a wide-eyed expression, a smile that seems to offer an apology. It's an open, Midwestern face that helps me understand how a person might decide to pitch irony altogether and buy a house and a lawn tractor and prepare to weather the last two-thirds of their life with someone capable of that look. This is a hell of a quagmire that Jamie's created, an ungainly mess with more potential victims than solutions. I asked him awhile back if he had an exit strategy. He didn't. Just a series of ill-defined hopes and ambitions, and a vague desire not to see anyone hurt, which is all well and good. But it's a bad situation, and I can't help but feel that by bringing me here he's made me a party to it. Not that I can hold that against Brenda. She seems like a very decent person who was open to the idea of love and happened to have the rotten luck of finding it with a married man.

Jamie comes crashing back out the screen door. Brenda asks, "Can I get you boys anything? Coffee? A glass of water?"

"Thanks, I'm fine," I say.

"Hey, look," Jamie says, "I guess we should get going. We've got a lot of work ahead of us. Brenda, honey, I'll bring some tools by later this week, maybe, fix that hole up." Brenda looks at the ground, kind of paws at it with her sandalled foot.

"That'd be so wonderful, Jimbo," she says, and then turns

to me. "Maybe we'll see each other again, then."

"Who knows?" I say. "It was good to meet you, Brenda."

Jamie blows her a kiss as we climb back into the van. He glows. "See you later, hon," he calls, then presses the button to roll up his window.

Decatur is a dying city. I'm looking at the rotted shells of warehouses and silos that dot the south end as we cruise by. Jamie sits silent for a long while.

Finally: "So, what do you think of her?"

"She seems real nice, Jamie."

"You see what I mean about her not being like Janet."

"Well, hmm. I guess. I mean, she's not your wife, so that's one real big difference right there."

"Fuck you," he says. "Fuck you, you fucking fuck."

This hurts, but not for the intended reason. It hurts because words like that used to roll out of Jamie, used to suit him, his defiant posture, his fearlessness—my brother would swear at anybody. Now he sounds like a father, or a teacher, someone who uses the words just to make sure he still knows them. That makes him old, and it makes me old.

It also suggests the gulf between who we were sure we would be, and who we have instead become. I feel this every day. I imagine Jamie does too—how could he not?—but probably doesn't expect me to feel it.

Of this I'm certain: the real differences between us are negligible, though we appear to represent two entirely different approaches to living. While he struggles to keep ahead of the yardwork, the sagging eaves, the minivan's oil changes, I come away looking collected. My black suits with their clean lines, my well-paying position with Witt-DeKalb Investments, my tidy, airy apartment near Lincoln Park in

Chicago, and the Moroccan and Nepalese restaurants I dine at, they all speak to something nearly opposite to Jamie's life here in Blue Mound. But the truth is that I have kept things small, manageable, in order to maintain the illusion of control. Jamie has allowed himself no such luxury. We want the same things, finally. We want the same woman, too; or at least we once did. I don't precisely know where Jamie stands on that issue these days. He is on the surface of things content with his duplicitous arrangement. Brenda Canty satisfies certain doubts he would otherwise harbour about himself, and she demands very little of him. A few hours carved from the corpus of his week, and the occasional nice dinner someplace dark in Springfield, if he can find the time. Though friendly and cheery, Brenda is frankly not the woman Janet is, but I suppose that's largely the point.

At the giant hardware store a yellow-haired girl rings up our sale, pointing a wireless scanner at the tags on the ends of the pieces of lumber, the brackets, the boxes of nails, the spackle and drywall patch kit, until the little unit beeps. When she's not using her hands she tucks them into her orange canvas apron. When finally she announces the total, it causes me to glance at the small digital screen atop the register to confirm I've heard right. Jamie, unblinking, slaps his credit card down on the counter. "Put that right on there," he says.

We wheel the orange cart full of lumber and supplies out into the parking lot and begin to load the van, folding the seats into the floor and then piling the eight-foot boards atop that, and right up between the driver and passenger seats. The tension that was present in the van before we went into the store has been replaced by a breezy feeling, a sense, perhaps bestowed by the giant hardware store, that *things are possible*, that *things can get done*. Between us now is an easy give and take, an attitude like *fuck it, it's the Memorial Day weekend, and the sun is out in America*. Our afternoon promises hammers and power tools and cold beer. I'll get a burn on my forearms. There will be barbecued hamburgers. The kids will climb trees. There is an obvious difference of opinions in the van about the Brenda thing, but we're not about to solve it, so we just leave it alone. Jamie starts up the motor, pops out the CD and turns on the radio. It's a sports talk station, and they're talking about baseball.

Jamie's loyalty to the Royals, here in the thick of Cubs and, to a lesser degree, White Sox territory, is no fluke. We were both born in Kansas City, but our father moved us up to Illinois so that he could manage a wholesale feed and seed outfit when I was six and Jamie was ten. Jamie can remember watching George Brett play, whereas I didn't form any sort of lasting allegiance until later, once we were already up here, so by that time it was Ryne Sandberg and the Cubs for me. It still is the Cubs, which marks me either a romantic or a fool. Take your pick.

It must be a hundred degrees under the early afternoon sun by the time we have the old porch stripped down and ready for rebuilding.

"Beer o'clock yet?" Jamie asks while hunched over a pair of sawhorses with a pencil in one hand and a tape measure in the other. The sweat pours over our faces, soaks through our shirts. Janet appears every now and then with a pitcher of ice water, then disappears again to the backyard where she's busy in the garden.

By 4:30 we have a new frame built, a lattice of two-by-fours strung between the four-by-fours we have carriage-bolted to the old posts, having decided that digging new postholes and pouring cement will make the job something bigger than we can reasonably expect to finish in two-and-a-half days. The old posts are rot-free, solid, and well rooted. They'll do. We set the new ones to level and bolt them in place, then build our frame off that.

The burgers are juicy and the beer cold as the early evening sun slants through the poplars. Voices float on the hot wind; it sounds as though the neighbours are having a barbecue, too. Children laugh and shout. The crickets start to chime in, like a ringing in the ears. Janet works the grill, making cheeseburgers with fried onions on toasted buns, potato salad rich with red onion and Miracle Whip. The ice in the beer cooler has all melted. My face is hot with sunburn, and somewhere a lawnmower whirs.

I can feel it in my muscles and bones: there will be no rooftop sitting this night. Jamie's been hitting the beer hard since we called it a day and packed the tools and lumber into the garage, stacked the old lumber in a neat pile out behind the garden shed. Now he's slumped low in his plastic deck chair, his face red as a beet, his eyelids heavy. The kids all but mind themselves nearby, spraying each other with the hose and splashing in the wading pool, which is full of water beneath a layer of grass clippings. Angela laughs; Robbie, ruddy and sodden, screams.

The longest shadows have reached the other side of the yard when Janet stands up, finishes the last of her beer and tells the kids to pack up their pool noodles. Time to get ready for bed. They moan, offer protest, and many minutes later follow her inside, wrapped in bright towels. The patio door closes behind them with a soft *whoosh*.

Jamie and I sit together in silence for a moment. He sighs deeply. "God, she's something, isn't she?" he asks cryptically.

The last of the sunset sweetens the western sky as he stands and picks up the cooler, retrieves the last four cans of Bud from the icy water, and dumps the rest of the contents off the side of the deck.

"I'm turning in early, brother," he says, teetering before the sliding door. "You good?"

"Yeah, I'm good. You sleep well," I say. "Back at it tomorrow."

"Yessir," he says, saluting. "Goodnight." He is off into the darkened house. I hear him walking past the bathroom where Janet is getting Robbie and Angela cleaned up for bed. I begin to gather condiments, glasses and plates from the patio table. Angela appears behind the screen of the patio door in a long pink nightgown with large-headed princesses on it.

"Goodnight, Uncle Richie," she says.

"Come here and gimme a hug before bed, Angie." She slides open the screen and pads across the deck into my waiting arms, and sinks into me. She smells of soap bubbles. She has her mother's dark hair.

"Sleep well, sweet Angie."

"I will," she says, then rubs her eyes and tiptoes away.

Her children and husband safely tucked away, Janet sits at the table in the darkened kitchen, a dish towel thrown over her left shoulder, a sweating can of beer in front of her. I stand leaning against the dishwasher. We are alone. She asks if I want a last beer, and I gratefully accept. It's the first time I've been alone with her this weekend. She looks tired. She stands, walks to the fridge and gets me a tallboy.

"Shoot, I could've gotten that, Jan," I say. The window over the sink is open and a cool breeze wafts through. Clouds have rolled in, blotting the stars. It has begun to rain softly, a light, cool shower that sounds like faint hissing from where I stand. It will be gone by morning, I know, and the sun will roll back out, burning off the dampness. Jamie and I will be back at it by mid-morning, sawing and hammering, measuring and cutting the decking boards, the long straight pieces of pressure-treated lumber that will mutely witness whatever does or does not happen to this family over the coming months and years. Janet will carry groceries over them. Robbie will skin his knees on them. Angela will escort friends across them. What will my brother do?

Janet is tired. I want to tell her everything I know about Jamie and Brenda.

"My god, those kids of yours have grown," I say.

"Like bad weeds," she says, then smiles. "They're good kids." We stand side by side in the kitchen and outside the rain falls. Janet's shoulders drop and she rubs the back of her neck with a rough hand, her nails still blackened with garden soil. In the dim light of the bulb in the range hood I notice the tiny lines beginning to creep outward from the corners of her eyes. "Robbie told me the other day that he wanted to sign up for basketball," she says. I think of Brenda Canty and imagine both women in the bleachers of a gymnasium, cheering Robbie on as he stands at the free throw line, neither aware of the other in the buzzing, yellowy light.

"Hope he's better than his dad was," I say.

She looks down at the linoleum tile, then gives herself a little hug, her arms folded across her stomach. I'm still looking at Janet's face, and I can't bring myself to speak. Maybe there was a time when I'd have moved in and held her now, consoled her from a sadness she doesn't quite realize she ought to be feeling. But that's not the way we live now.

Truth is I don't even know what I'd say. *Jesus Christ*, I think to myself, *he's my brother*. Janet pushes herself away from the counter and stands straight, pulls her shoulders back to work out an ache. She looks straight at me with her hazel eyes.

"You got what you need, Richie?"

"I guess I do," I say.

"Alright then," she says, then slaps the dishtowel down on the counter and turns off the light over the stove. "I'm off to bed. Jim'll wonder where I'm at." Then she moves silently down the hall and into the bedroom.

IN THE FOOTHILLS

Marty came down out of the mountains in early March, trailing a string of bad decisions. He started high up in the Rockies and swept into Calgary, coasting at great speed, like his brake lines had been cut.

I was working in a big sporting goods store, selling skis and running shoes and golf clubs. I had been thinking about heading back to Ontario, but that would've required putting my tail between my legs, and I wasn't ready for that just yet.

He'd been married to my sister for a short time, before she cracked up. My mother still says Eileen's "taken ill." Most recently Marty had been in Hundred Mile House, doing I don't know what, exactly. The details were vague. Before that he'd been in Vancouver. Trouble trailed him like a wake; bad ideas poured off him like a stench. Every time I saw him he was driving a different car. Not new cars, but different ones. This time it was a blue Cavalier with lightning bolts down the sides.

Since he and Eileen split and she walked herself into an emergency room wearing a nightgown, Marty has drifted like pollen from place to place, his welding papers in his back pocket. He'd stay for a time, use up his luck, then move on to the next town. He'd done like that after he got out of the Air Force at Cold Lake, but then he met Eileen and they had a couple of years where they imitated normal people, settled in one place, rented a nice house east of the city. They stayed in nights. Then real colours began to show through and things went haywire, like I'd felt they would.

Since then he and I have kept in touch, in a fashion, and all the while I've battled feelings of guilt for some sort of disloyalty to my sister. But then again I have since childhood suspected my sister to be the cause of all bad things.

Marty is big. Not obese, just large, built on a different scale than most human beings. He stands about six-foot-four, and his limbs are like telephone poles. His torso is like the front of a transport truck, and on his feet he wears a size thirteen or fourteen pair of boots. When he drinks, which he often does, it's usually from something big, a jar or a big plastic travel coffee mug. He drinks vodka mostly, Russians or screwdrivers. Drinks them like water. Sometimes the only way you can tell he's on his way down is that his face and neck get beet red. Eventually he just collapses. Finds a bed or a sofa and you can forget about Marty for twelve hours or so.

The thing with Marty is, when he comes to stay with you, there's no way of knowing how long he'll be there. He arrived on a Saturday afternoon and immediately went to sleep on the futon in the other room, the room that had been empty since my roommate skipped out on me. Marty stayed there until midday Sunday. I could hear him snoring. Once or twice in the night I heard him get up to use the bathroom, a bear of a man, a lumberjack shaking the whole apartment as he moved, then planting his feet before the toilet and uncorking a torrent. Water running, then slow, heavy footsteps back down the hallway, the sound of a California redwood being felled as he tumbled back into bed, and then nothing, just faint sawing for hours and hours thereafter.

A chinook had followed Marty down from the hills, and Sunday was a warm, springy day, a breeze alive with smells where the day before it had been cold and dead. By Sunday noon it was a beaut of a day, the sun at its full strength, the sound of water running off the roofs, everything slick. I could sit at my window and watch the snowbanks below melting like ice cubes in an empty glass. I'd opened the windows and was listening to CCR when Marty emerged from the second bedroom. I always listen to CCR when winter turns to spring, and even if this was a false beginning, I needed to feel good about things after the winter I'd had.

"What in the hell are you doing?" he asked me.

"Polishing my boots," I said. I was standing hunched over the table where I'd spread out newspapers, some spare rags, and an old shoebox containing my polish kit: a tin of polish, two brushes, and a shining rag.

"Look at you, your highness!"

"Sunday," I said. "Every Sunday I polish my boots. My dad used to do it."

"I see," he said, then looked around, sniffed, and rubbed his stomach. The smell of polish must have reminded him of the smell of food.

"Got any vittles here?" he asked.

"Sure, yeah. Cereal, toast..."

"Eggs? Bacon? Potatoes?"

"Yeah," I said, "though the potatoes might have sprouted."

"All right then, you do your thing, I'll cook." And he did. He went to work in my pathetic little kitchen, and with a cutting board, a dull knife, and a single fry pan he beavered away until he had made us a rich spread of eggs and bacon, toast, beans, and warm stewed tomatoes. When my plate was empty he refilled it. Only once I was done did Marty sit down and eat. He had thirds, finished everything. I had forgotten this about Marty, that he loved to spend time in the kitchen, and that Eileen never had to cook.

By mid-afternoon, still full, we were sitting on the couch sharing my cigarettes, the sliding door to the patio wide open to let in the sweet warm breeze. CCR had given way to Rush in the five-disc changer: Marty's choice.

"What time do you work tomorrow?" he asked me.

"One," I said. "One 'til close."

"Good, then you can sleep in," he said, lighting another.

"Why do I need to sleep in?"

"There's a bar I think we should close tonight," he said. "Passed it on the way here."

And I thought, why not? What's the worst that can happen to me, in the company of this man who'd cooked me such a generous meal, on a Sunday night in the foothills with the warm breath of springtime upon me?

"Let's do that," I said.

We took my truck, the truck I drove out to Alberta from Kingston, the truck that I lived in for two weeks until I found an apartment. It occurred to me that there was no definite plan as to what we might do with the truck, how we might get back to my apartment or, failing that, where we would stay after this night of drinking. It's something I felt that we were actively not discussing, a thing floating between us. I kept returning to it in my head, but deciding that I shouldn't bring it up, because I felt like Marty was daring me to do just that, to be the responsible one, so that he could be proven, in a single chop, the opposite. Marty defined himself by these sorts of oppositions.

We drove west, straight toward the Rockies, which loomed purple and holy before us, an unreal painted backdrop. The last of the sun was honey oozing between the peaks, and through it we moved slowly, lazily. In the middle distance the foothills burped up from the prairie, little practice runs, junior topography. That's where we were headed, to a place called the Starlite, located nowhere in particular, just a sign, a parking lot, and a roadhouse.

We stood in the parking lot, Marty and I, feeling—what? Apprehension? Excitement? It's likely, given what transpired later, that we were not feeling the same thing at that moment, though it felt for all the world that we were comrades, men linked by uneven pasts and a hope that the near future, namely this night, would prove to be a kind one.

We leaned against the truck and did some damage to a six-pack liberated from my fridge. The light disappeared and the night came on and we watched two or three trucks pull in, their drivers making their way to the Starlite's steel door with their heads down.

My hair plastered down and my boots newly polished, I felt like a handsome devil. Maybe there'd be women inside, I thought. That's why I had come, for drinks and whatever interesting faces this evening might invite in. The usual things. I assumed that's why Marty had brought us out there, an assumption I'd find to be false in due time.

Marty specialized in broken women: those who'd known bad men, bad times, those who'd become familiar with the youth justice system. That's what drew him to my sister, of course. She hadn't yet gone off the rails, but he saw something in her. Marty would ride their momentum for a time, have some laughs, then jump off before things completely fell apart. He had a knack for it. When you were riding alongside Marty you would meet women who quickly began to tell you about themselves—everything in one sitting—and you'd hear some crazy things. Then they'd want you to commend them on their strength, given all they'd endured. Sometimes I'd say something along the lines of, "Well, we've all got trouble, sweetness, but we don't necessarily go blabbing it to the first person we meet in a bar." This stance had, on more than one occasion, hurt Marty's chances with certain women, and he openly discouraged me from adopting it, or at least voicing it. I'd try to comply, if only because part of me felt that I owed Marty something.

An explanation on that one: while duck hunting with borrowed guns three years earlier, I broke my tibia galloping down a slope toward the spot we'd selected, on the rim of a broad marsh. Marty tied a stick to my leg and then put me on his shoulder and carried me three kilometres back to the truck. He let me drain the vodka from his flask while he drove me to the hospital. An episode like that can endear a person to you, even in the face of their obvious shortcomings.

I was remembering all this as we stood outside the Starlite. I could hear the wind, which had taken on a coolness I didn't welcome, and I could hear the bar's sign buzzing. Far out in the night I could hear traffic on the highway, transports moving between Calgary and the mountains, and Vancouver beyond that, though at that moment the road in front of us was empty.

"Don't see his truck," Marty muttered, lifting his bottle to his lips.

"Whose truck?" I asked, but Marty was pitching his bottle across the gritty parking lot and striding toward the Starlite's front door. If he heard me he ignored the question.

Inside it was dark and musty with a checkerboard linoleum floor that might once have been black and white, but had gone grey and yellow many years ago. There were about a dozen patrons scattered about, most of them in high-backed booths, while three men in plaid shirts and leather vests slumped over the bar. The walls were wood panelled, but the chintzy variety of wood panelling, the kind your dad might have installed in your basement. It was warped in several spots. It had been a year or two since they'd gotten rid of smoking everywhere, but you could still smell the stale tobacco coming out of the Starlite's every plank and fibre. I imagined the bar stools' stuffing exhaling it every time another ass hammered down on them.

Marty strode to the bar and took a stool, and I followed. The man behind the bar wasn't very interested in our being there. He was having a conversation with one of the other men sitting at the bar. But in a moment he came to us and we ordered beers. Above the bartender's head a small television perched on a wobbly looking shelf played a hockey game. The Flames were in L.A. The men at the bar were looking up at that through their eyebrows.

We slumped over the bar and half watched the hockey game and drank beer for an hour or so. There wasn't much conversation between us. Just quiet drinking. Then Marty stood up and excused himself to the men's.

I watched him go in the mirror over the bar. Then a moment later I watched that big steel door open and let in a blast of cool air. Riding it were a strange pair, a man and a woman, she taller than him, who nodded to the bartender, then walked past me to a booth in the corner. As they passed me I could smell them: she wore flowery perfume, and he smelled sourly and pungently of pot. They took off their coats and hung them on hooks near the mouth of their booth. The man came to the bar, chatted with the keeper, and got them a pitcher of beer and a couple of glasses.

The man wore a knit Rastafarian hat, green, yellow, red, beneath which lay a long, dark ponytail. He wore an open plaid shirt with a black T-shirt underneath, from the front of which smiled Mr. Bob Marley.

The woman was tall and thin. If they were to make a movie about this whole incident they'd probably cast Katherine Heigl to play her, and that could work but only if Katherine Heigl was falling apart a bit. The skin of the woman's face was sagging a little, her elbows were bony, and her hair looked sort of like straw. But she was still pretty, there was no seeing around that. Probably as pretty or prettier a woman as either Marty or I would ever know again. She looked nice in her jeans, and she was a good three or four inches taller than Bob Marley. It was obvious to everyone present that our little Bob was punching well above his weight.

They settled into their booth and I more or less forgot about them. Marty was taking his sweet time, I thought, and a moment later I saw the light leak out from the bathroom door as it swung open. Marty's path back to our stools took him right by Bob and Broken Katherine, and on the way by he said, loud enough for the whole bar to hear, "Good to see you again, asshole!"

Why would he have done that? I wondered.

Marty fell down onto his stool and I could smell the drink on him. I realized that he'd lapped me several times over in terms of consumption. He was close to drunk; if he wasn't already there, he was on the outskirts. I thought maybe that had something to do with his greeting to Bob Marley.

"How do you feel tonight?" he boomed at me.

"I feel pretty good, Marty," I said.

"That's good. That's frickin' good," he said. "I gotta say, though, our evening might be about to change."

"How so, Marty?"

"I might have to beat that little guy to death," he said, and he was smiling broadly. His face was red, his ears and his neck. Something was racing through him.

"Why's that, Marty?"

"Oh, that don't frickin' matter now," he said, and he swivelled around to face the bar. He was finishing a beer and then he ordered a shot of vodka. Then a second.

"You want anything?" he asked me, but I just tilted my half-full glass to show its contents. "Fair enough," he said.

After a third shot he spun back around and faced the corner where the couple sat. He was looking at them over my shoulder and grinning. He watched them a moment and he moved his mouth like he was looking for something to say. He chuckled to himself.

"You need a ladder to kiss her?" he shouted.

"Fuck you," someone shouted back, but it didn't seem to me that it was Bob. He might have a defender in this, I remember thinking.

"How do you fuck her?" Marty shouted to the whole barroom.

I wished to hide then in my glass of beer. "Marty," I asked, "do you know those two?"

"I might've run into them before. Here." Then he laughed like a clown might before it touches you in the funhouse.

"On the way into town, am I right?" I asked.

"Sure, sure," Marty said. Then he shouted, "Look at him! Look at you! You look like her kid brother!" The couple was trying their best to ignore all of this. I don't imagine they were successful. Everyone else in the Starlite had gone quiet, like villagers waiting for a bombing run to end.

"You don't talk much," he said to me.

"I don't have much to say," I responded. "Not much important, anyway. I don't really know what's going on here."

"What's frickin' going on here is that I stopped by for a sip on Saturday afternoon, stopped right here at this establishment, and I was enjoying myself, talking to blondie there. Seemed to me we were getting on great. Then her fella there comes in and starts saying some unkind things, and I got agitated because it seemed to me that if he and I were laid out on a buffet, at best he'd be an appetizer, where I'd be the main course. I could see she might feel that way too, and I was about to do something about it when I was advised that the gentleman a few stools down was a police officer. That changed my plans somewhat. So I said I'd come back and we'd finish."

"And you brought me."

"You weren't busy, were you?"

"Suppose not."

After Marty's speech I decided I'd have a double Canadian Club, no ice, and as I ordered that I happened to glance in the mirror and notice their booth had gone empty.

Then I heard a microsecond of shouting. My jaw went electric and the stool I'd been sitting on was suddenly beside and above me. Marty's head was nearly staved in by the thick glass bottom of an empty pitcher, whereas I think Katherine Heigl had walloped me with a plate.

There were shattered bits of light in my eyes, on the floor. The linoleum down there smelled of winter and salt.

I was still trying to move my face when I heard Marty get to his feet and start to shuffle after our Bonnie and Clyde, who'd retreated to the other side of the room. Bob Marley was holding a stool in front of him and Marty, whose face was bloody, was headed over there with his fists loaded. But the bartender shouted, "Hey!" and when I could see over the bar I noticed the shotgun in his hands. There wasn't any doubting who it was pointed at. In fact the whole room of people was lined up against Marty and, to a lesser degree, me. Clearly the other two had thrown the first, but they were local and we weren't. We weren't even Albertans. And we probably didn't vote the same way either. They had their reasons is what I'm getting at.

"Christ!" Marty shouted, then reached down to yank me up. When we got to the truck it just worked out that I climbed into the driver's seat, though I had no business being there. I felt like someone had packed cotton balls into my skull. There was a sharp pain where my teeth ought to have been and I couldn't speak.

In my dreams of that happier life, things like this were securely in my past. They weren't adventures to me anymore; they caused my heart to ache. I'd look at myself and shake my head. That happier life—the hope of it, the possibility of it—came to me in sparing moments now, like when I'd eaten that breakfast Marty had made, or when we stood in the blue twilight in the Starlite's parking lot and it seemed like maybe we had a good evening ahead of us. But every time one of those moments sprang up it was gone again just as fast, and that happy life got further and further away, like a thing you watch blow away in a storm.

It was full-on night now, the roads bare but for my sweeping headlights. I didn't feel as though I was driving, but rather that the truck was driving me. I felt safe. That's why it was so surprising to me when that tree came up. I thought, who'd put a tree there? But of course it was that we'd left the road behind. The truck wasn't saving us, and Marty reached over for the steering wheel. He was saying something but I couldn't hear it because of the wind whistling in the hole where the windshield used to be.

There was an interval when I was aware of darkness, but not of anything else. I don't know if I was conscious or not, or just what state I was in. When I came to and tried to open my eyes there was a dazzling spray of light. What was interesting was that I couldn't be sure if the light originated inside my head or if it came from somewhere else. I know there was a helicopter, and quickly reckoned that I must be in it. The copter's blades sounded like a series of pops. *Pop-pop-pop-pop*, in a sort of fast slow motion. With each pop it felt as though my head might implode. I tried to look at myself but came to find that I was strapped down. I wanted then to throw up because my feet were above my head and the level earth was a distant memory.

I wondered about my truck, and in fact I must have asked aloud, because someone said it was gone. I thought that was too bad, because I felt a great sense of loyalty to that blue 1988 GMC, the truck that Marty had driven to the hospital after our ill-fated duck expedition, as I sat in the passenger seat and my head lolled around like a pinball and the pain felt like it had a centre and a million radiant arms. Our borrowed shotguns rattled around in the bed. It had been a good truck.

My blood felt milky. The helicopter rose and rose, as though it was going to take me over the mountains, or into the clouds. What happened then was that I had a flashback to the moment before we'd left the road, Marty and I, in my blue truck. I had been thinking that sometimes your life isn't the one you want to be living, even if it isn't terrible or dire. There was nothing I wouldn't mind seeing the end of, I had said to myself. That included Marty.

Now in the ascending helicopter, still going up, I didn't know if Marty was alive or dead, and I didn't want to ask. I knew he wasn't nearby, in my helicopter, but maybe he was in his own, thumping similarly heavenward. I wondered if we'd both wake up in the same ward, a mint-green curtain separating our mechanical beds, and laugh about all this. But I hoped not. I hoped I wouldn't see Marty on the other side of this. It was all his doing; I couldn't see it any other way. My head was enduring a slow explosion and my eyes didn't seem to be working quite right. The rest of my body was at that moment either a rumour or a memory and I had to face the reality that Alberta wasn't really working out for me. And goddamn Marty, I thought. The mountains had sent him, and it was my great desire that the mountains should take him back.

JAMBOREE

Buddy of mine set me up with three or four days of work doing security at the Havelock Country Jamboree. Under the table pay. Fifty thousand people camping in a field, drinking and listening to country music. I stood near a fence and nodded at concertgoers as they walked by flashing their wristbands. By the time it got dark that first night, though, I was feeling pretty useless, so I started to get drunk. I found Cub and he came by and we started getting drunk together, standing by that fence.

Cub said, "Rupert, do you even like Trace Adkins?" Cub wouldn't have known what to say if I'd asked him what he was doing there, so I didn't.

I said, "Call Frank. Let's go see Steven."

We've all got sadness like a rot in the timbers, but Steven's the only one who ever did anything about it. So now, every once in a while, we take a couple of bottles and go visit him where he lies beneath an elm tree in the Marmora Common Cemetery.

Cub texted Frank and Frank said he was in. Cub and I filled our pockets with cans and found his car. I said, "Can you drive?" and Cub said, "Can I drive." I said, "What are you drinking?" He had a can of those things that taste like melted popsicles.

"It says," he said, studying the can as we passed beneath a floodlight, "SOPHISTICATED VODKA COOLER."

"Pretty sure anything actually sophisticated doesn't need to have 'sophisticated' written on it," I said.

"Look, though," he said, tapping the can, "palm trees."

"Oh, right," I said, "that establishes it."

I don't know how late it was. I was kind of bombed. But the night felt a lot like the time we were far enough gone that we'd got it in our heads to dig Steven up. That night time felt wispy, a thing rolled out in front of us, a thing that got longer and longer as we scraped and dug, but also shorter and thinner, like it could just disappear.

I hoped we wouldn't try that again—digging him up. Frank had used his pocketknife to cut the sod and somewhere approaching dawn they found me on my knees hacking away at the dirt with Cub's mom's gardening trowel. I think we got down a foot, maybe eighteen inches. Being caught might not have been so embarrassing if we'd actually managed to dig a decent hole.

Frank was already there. The easiest thing to do is to park at the Valu-Mart right next to the cemetery and climb up the hill. Frank's Civic was parked there under the light, and he was leaning against the driver's side door, smoking a cigarette. Frank has a moustache like a janitor and prescription glasses shaped like aviators, with heavy lenses tinted brown.

The air was thick and fragrant as honey. Frank said, "I feel like a bag of glass."

Cub said, "You look like a bag of shit."

The sadness is something you think you can get out ahead of, maybe once life opens up a bit, once things settle down some. But that never happens, and eventually the sadness gathers you in and you become a part of it, and it of you, so that there's no separating the two. Steven knew that.

He and I worked two years side by side installing roofs. I mostly enjoyed it, felt like being up there and looking down on things gave me some perspective on my life. It made the big, scary things seem smaller, like I could get above, and so maybe beyond them. Steven felt differently.

We crested the little hill and walked among the rows of stones. The grass gave off a wet coolness, and the stones seemed to radiate cold air into the warm night. We moved toward the big elm. In the slight wind it gave off a hissing like tires on a wet road.

We found Steven's plot and just sort of stood around him. We kept away and to the sides, like he was lying on top of the grass and we didn't want to step on him. Cub saluted, then walked around the other side of the elm to take a piss. Frank smoked.

"Sometimes I'm angry with him," I said. "Sometimes, you know, the things he'd say."

Cub called, "I hear you." It's healthy, we believe, to say the things you feel, even to the dead. We tell Steven, or say in his presence, exactly what we feel.

"He could run his mouth, yes," Frank said, "but the whole Toronto thing? You did that to yourself. Don't pin that on Steven."

"There was no job," I said. "I got there and I said 'I'm here for the job' and they looked at me like I was a fucking idiot. I moved everything I owned, Frank."

"You threw a chair at the HR guy," Frank said. "Steven didn't make you throw that chair."

"I was upset," I said. "I was upset with you, Steven."

Cub tossed his cooler can away. It landed a couple of rows over and skipped off a headstone.

"You should pick that up," Frank told him. "It's disrespectful."

"I'll get it on my way out," Cub said, pulling a new can out of the pocket of his hooded sweatshirt. Frank and I shuffled a bit, looking over at the can where it landed.

Things half done, things done poorly, the things we fail to maintain. That's where you see it. There are no ways around it. My grass is never cut. My car leaks oil. All the girls not kissed. All those TV series I never stuck it out to see the end of.

We stood around not saying anything for a time. The wind knocked things together and cars whipped past on Highway 7. The light from the Valu-Mart parking lot lip up the western end of the cemetery like a movie set.

"I still can't get my head around that he's down there," I said. "Like, him. Steven."

"Only not him," Cub said.

"You know what we should do, don't you?" Frank said. "We should do it again. Finish it this time." He was sitting on a stone nearby with his arms folded over his chest, holding his smoke in front of his face with two fingers.

"Do it again?" I said.

"Yeah. Get him out, let him breathe a bit."

Cub said, "Hell, yes."

I said, "I feel like that's a bad thing to do. I don't know. Like if we're caught there's probably already a note on our record about the last time and they'll see that and so we'll be kind of fucked."

"There's no note," Frank said.

"Maybe there's a note," said Cub, "but I don't care. Fuck the note."

"Fuck the note," said Frank. "But there's no note."

"No note?" I said. Cub was already toeing the grass near Steven's marker. Frank's arms were still folded across his chest, but something in the set of his mouth looked to me like a challenge.

So we started to dig him up again. This time, though, we had a decent shovel. Frank's an electrician and always has a trunk full of tools. I don't think he generally carries a spade, but this night he had one. He went down to his car, out front the grocery store, and he came back with it. He put the point of the blade into the soft turf and stepped up on the curled rim of it. The word "premeditation" bounced around inside my skull, as did the word "decomposition."

There was a field behind me, and country music, a kind of bullshit good time hokum, people dancing in stupid hats, people sitting in lawn chairs keeping time on their knees, people having sex behind porta-potties. I could hear it all, though of course I couldn't really hear any of it. It was fifteen minutes down 7, or a hundred miles away, or a thousand. But it was there, in my ears, as Frank's spade cut the sod and Cub stood holding his can of vodka cooler. How do people have fun, I wondered.

I stood dumb while Frank began the work and soon there was a small hole there, about three feet from the base of Steven's stone. This is my opportunity to stop this, I told myself, if what I really want to do is stop it.

But I didn't do anything. I was silent. And while I said nothing I thought about how for about ten years I hadn't done anything because doing something felt like opening myself up to more sadness.

The hole was getting bigger, and I realized that was what I wanted. For that hole to get bigger and bigger.

Frank worked like a machine for the duration of the first shift, breaking into a sweat as he found a rhythm that actually lulled me. I don't know how long he was at it. It might have been fifteen minutes and it might have been an hour, but I know that at the end of it Cub bounced up and grabbed the shovel and dove right in, though it was obvious from his first stroke that he wasn't really anticipating just how laborious a thing it was. He was a fair bit slower than Frank.

Eventually it was my turn. The earth smelled so rich, so earthy, so full of nutrients and life. It made a lovely sound against the blade as the shovel bit in and I pulled hard and lifted such weight that the wood of the shovel's handle gave a soft little squeak. I hoisted it above and to my right, feeling my shoulders burn and my right elbow twinge as though it might give way. My palms were red and pregnant with blisters.

Steven was down there, and by this time I had in my head notions that we'd be freeing him from something unpleasant, some bothersome life he'd be pleased to escape for a short time. We were doing him a favour.

"We'll take him to the Jamboree," I said between breaths, leaning on the shovel.

"Ha! Just, like, prop him up in the back seat with a wristband on, then get him out and walk him around," Cub said. "That'd be so real. So, so real."

"Steven wasn't a real big Wynonna Judd fan," said Frank. "I don't think he'd be so hot on that idea."

"Just to be out," I said, "to see people. To feel things."

"Well," said Cub, "we'll just get him out, let him breathe. See what we feel like doing then."

Sweat poured from me. Cub disappeared a moment, I heard his car's door open and then shut, and he came back with more coolers tucked into his pockets. He handed me one and I gratefully took it. Cherry-pear-melon, or something. Cracked open, it smelled like summer. I drained it, then placed the can on the lip of the hole, which was now a good four feet deep. I gripped the shovel again and drove it into the dirt.

Damp, fuzzy light from the parking lot lamps filtered through the trees and fell on us, fell on the gravestones, the grass. In that light we were beautiful and tragic, all three of us. Sweat dripped from us like baptism water. Cub looked like a baby. A man shaped like a baby. Frank looked like a sage. Quiet and wise. I felt pure. Oh, hell, I'll say it: I felt like a saint.

I've always felt that labour had a way of washing me clean, scraping me down, making me somehow more whole. Like I could sweat out the bad with the poisons. This—digging up Steven's body—fit with that.

The only dead body I'd ever seen in the wild, which is to say not in a funeral home or church, belonged to a freshly killed boy from our high school who'd bolted out onto the road for some reason, right out front the school, and been clipped by a Dodge Ram and then lay there on the pavement while the life quickly drained from him. A dozen of us watched this happen from the sidewalk, the Smoking Section, we called it. A girl named Lindsay buried her face in my chest while I watched the boy—his name was Chris, he was in grade nine—lay there and die. That was a strange moment for me, because while I didn't want to see Chris or anybody else get killed, I was very glad that Lindsay Matthews was touching me. A couple of people went over to Chris, and a teacher came out, then the principal. Traffic stopped. An ambulance came. But he was dead. I'd seen his face, which was toward us, slacken and go blank. The skin hung loose there, his mouth wide open. But he was still obviously a person, because everything was in the right place, eyes, nose, hair, ears. A person, but suddenly without life.

I knew Steven wouldn't look like that. I knew there'd be a lot less of him, and that what was left wouldn't look like Steven. What is left, I wanted to know. What's down there that made him Steven?

The closer we got the more it began to feel like a ceremony we were performing, a ritual of some kind. A happy thing, I almost want to say. I climbed out of the hole and handed Frank the shovel and I said, "When we get closer we should call Nancy. She'll want to see him."

Nancy is Steven's mother. She used to be the receptionist at the high school. It was her voice you'd hear doing the announcements. Four-foot-ten. She'd let us smoke cigarettes in Steven's room. Now she watches fourteen hours of television and calls it a day.

"Nancy would want to know," agreed Frank, "but she wouldn't want to see him like he is. We'll call her tomorrow."

"What about Sarah?" said Cub, and my brain began fogging up. Sarah is Steven's sister, younger by two years, and so devastatingly beautiful to me that the thought of her caves my chest in still. We dated for a year and a half before Steven put an extension cord around his neck. Our love did not survive that. A few months later she moved to Toronto, and what she did there I do not know.

"You still talk to Sarah?" I asked Cub.

"Sometimes," he said.

Frank said, "Maybe Sarah." Then he took the shovel and slid down into the hole. I held my hand out toward Cub and he tossed me another vodka cooler. The shovel bit into the earth, the sugary, liquory syrup sloshed down my throat, I stared up at the elm tree, at the place where it met the dark, and I thought of Sarah.

She was twenty and I was twenty-two and how do you know then what you want? You don't know anything. I knew only that my favourite things in the world were the skin on the side of Sarah's neck—the way it felt on my lips, the way it smelled—and drinking beer at quitting time on a Friday afternoon with Steven.

As Frank dug again I eased myself down into the damp grass and leaned back against the stone of a man named Albert Crowe. Cub was holding a can in one hand and playing with his phone in the other.

"Don't call Sarah," I said to him.

"Okay," he said, and grinned.

"What?"

"I won't call her. But I already texted her."

"I wish you hadn't done that," I said.

Shortly before Steven did what he did, Sarah and I were in Norwood for the fall fair. It was early September and summer was ending. The night had that sweet, fine edge to it, where I knew it could just tip over and spill out at any moment. My hair was freshly cut, so I could feel the night air on my neck. She was wearing her hair down, tight jeans and a jean jacket. She still had sunglasses sitting atop her head. Sandalled feet, toenails freshly painted a deep, shining red. We'd spent an hour or two in my car, talking, listening to the radio, kissing. Finally, somewhere near 10:00, we got out of the car and walked over to the front gate of the fair. There was a security guard there. I said, "How much do we owe you for admission?" He said, "Sorry, we're closing up, I can't let you in."

He was seventeen, maybe eighteen. This was his first job, I could see it. He was short and solidly-built, probably played hockey or football, maybe both. His white short-sleeved shirt was tucked into his baggy black cargo pants. The patches on his chest and shoulder read SECURITY. I said, "Come on, I'll give you ten bucks, just let us walk around a bit."

He smiled shyly and said, "Sorry, sir, I can't let you in." The walkie-talkie on his belt crackled.

I balled my fists, tied the muscles of my forearms into knots. Sarah put her hand on my shoulder. The lights of the fair—the Ferris wheel, the Tilt-a-Whirl, the Gravitron, the Pirate Ship—all shone up into the hazy night air, making a luminescent cup over our heads. They were still racing tractors over by the grandstand. We could hear them, and we could faintly smell the exhaust, mixing with the scents of popcorn and cigarette smoke, the grass beneath our feet, and the damp, cooling night air. The lightest mist had begun falling.

"Come on, man," I said, "just let us in."

"Sorry, sir." Sarah's hand was in mine, though she didn't usually like to hold hands, and I could feel her whole body tensing up. She was staring up into the lights, at all the fun to be had on the other side of a flimsy string of plastic snow fencing. The security boy stood then with his hands on his hips, as though to make himself appear bigger.

What had been a lark, a laugh—the fair on a Saturday night—now felt like necessity, like direst, darkest need.

"Come on," said Sarah, pulling on my hand, "it's okay."

I turned my back to the gate and looked her in the eye, and I whispered, "How fast do you think he can run?"

She smiled and said again, "It's okay. Rupert? We'll find

something else to do," then she squeezed my hand. We began to walk away. Security boy said, "Goodnight. Sorry." The Norwood Fair rang on behind us. Lights flashed, tractor engines revved, rides spun and shot up and dropped suddenly. People screamed and laughed, music played. The whole scene seemed a bit unreal, the way it lit up the darkness. We walked along the wrong side of the fence, divided from a hot dog stand and an exhibit of stock cars, and I worried that what had happened was that my courage had abandoned me. What if we had run? What if we had hopped that fence?

Sarah held my hand still, and she seemed determined to make something good happen. She smiled at me, said again that it was fine. We walked and soon we were past the end of the fence and among houses, quiet and dark, and I was certain things would be fine, because I was with her. But the moment felt instructive: it felt like proof that the world would not let us in. It would not grant us admission. We'd arrived late, and so would have to find our own pleasure.

She looked me in the eye then, gave me a sly little smile, and led me by the hand. We walked down the road, crossed one last street, and then out into the wet grass of a field beyond. It was dark there, and she turned and threw herself at me. Soon we were in that grass, my jacket laid down like a blanket, her on her back, and me sort of in disbelief. She went for my belt and I have to tell you, it was like the Norwood Fair had just never existed at all.

"You texted her?" I said to Cub.

"Yup." Sometimes you just want to hit Cub.

"Jesus," I said. "What did you say?"

"I just said we were doing this."

"Let me see." He ambled around to my side of the hole and

fiddled a bit with his phone, then handed it to me. I read this:

Me: We r digging steven up
Sarah Wiggins: Again?
Me: Yup
Sarah Wiggins: Sure. Send me a pic.
Me: Will do
Sarah Wiggins: Serious?

And that was it. I wasn't sure from the way it left off if Sarah was expecting to hear from Cub again, or if that was the close of the conversation, if she'd decided this late night nugget was just more of Cub's usual bullshit. I looked at it again and saw that the time on the messages was after 3:00. So that's where we were, somewhere between three and four in the morning. I couldn't have told you that otherwise.

I looked at it once more, at the few words she'd typed, and I felt awful and small. I felt lost. I tossed Cub his phone. "Hey!" he said.

"I wish you hadn't done that," I said again, then leaned harder into Crowe's headstone and felt my heart spinning as I thought of Sarah's eyes and hair. Sadness came down over me like a mist.

About three weeks after the night at the fair, Steven did what he did. The next morning we all got that phone call. Sarah and I hung on for a few more weeks, through the funeral and such, but by mid-November we just couldn't. She was a ghost, a wisp. She'd walk in the room and drag herself through it and wouldn't know I was there. Her eyes got darker.

She said, "I can't be with you anymore," and I was nearly destroyed. It ruined me. I drank myself under, came up for air for a day or two, then sank again. I remember Frank saying to me, "The sun sets on everything." I said, "I wish you'd kill me, Frank, because I can't do it myself."

He said, "I love you, Rupert, but you're not worth the jail time."

Eight years later and here we were, digging Steven up. What the hell, he was there every day anyway. He was always there, sitting in on conversations, making us feel the way we did. We might as well look him in his empty eyes.

It was my turn to dig again. Frank tossed the shovel onto the grass and hauled himself up, sprawled his arms on the ground and kicked his legs until he could push himself out of the hole. He stood and handed me the shovel, and I slid back down.

The smell of the dirt had changed. In the air hung traces of our exertion, and the slow rotting smell of, I hate to think, the death all around us. It was cooler down there, and damp. I saw a rock peeking from the side of the hole and I thought it was a skull, which caused me to jump a bit.

When I bent to drive the spade into the dirt, the ground was at eye level. A plastic Valu-Mart shopping bag blew between the stones like a tiny ghost. I said to myself, this is what it's like to be dead.

I dug for ages. The sky lightened just a bit, the darkness growing fainter. I had sweat through my shoes. Earlier, as I watched Frank on his first shift, I saw a triangle of sweat darken his white T-shirt between his shoulder blades, I had thought this would be a bit of hard work, but not too bad. After all, I'd spent time carrying bundles of asphalt shingles up ladders and across roofs under murderous summer suns. But now, down there, in the close but cooling night, my socks were squelching and my hair was plastered to my face. The dirt clung to my damp skin, and every shovel heaping with dirt weighed a thousand pounds.

I got us close. With each pitch and shove of the blade I

thought it was imminent, that hard thing just beneath the surface. I worried about going right through soft wood, my shovel meeting Steven square where the bridge of his nose used to be. But I hit nothing, and eventually I ceded my duties.

"So close," said Cub. "I can feel it. He's right there." I tilted the shovel's handle toward him and he grimaced. "I think Frank should," he said. "I'm pretty spent." So I tilted the smooth wooden shaft toward Frank, who reached out and grabbed it, muttering, "You lazy little shit."

Questions flew around in my head like bats at dusk, screeching toward me but mostly unseen. I tried to grab them, because I felt like these questions were very important, that we should probably address them before lifting that final shovel full of dirt. But we were getting nearer and nearer to him, and Frank was chugging along now, a machine, an excavator. Cub was shirtless, standing on the rim of the hole, cheering, with his arms raised above his round head. There was no time. No time to stop, no time to talk, no time to prepare ourselves.

Were we trying to bring him to us, or to bring ourselves closer to Death?

Should we expect him to still have the long, thick hair he'd had in life?

Could I stand to see his straight, white teeth gone yellow with death and burial?

Within a few minutes the shovel gave a thick, flat thudding noise. "Jesus," said Cub.

"Well, boys," Frank said, and then nothing else. He leaned the shovel against the side of the hole, got down on his knees, and started using his hands. I could hear his breathing, a mix of windedness and fear.

The first birds were starting to sound. In a few more minutes Frank had cleared away all the dirt from the top of the box, a black casket that I remembered from where it stood in the funeral home, heavy and ominous. It was duller in sheen now, lying beneath the earth, but no less heart-stopping. There were silver accents, lines and finials, along the edges and corners. They still shone in places, catching traces of light.

Would the top be locked or clasped?

Would we have to break the thing wide open, smash it apart, to drag him out?

Would he come out in one piece, or would things begin falling off of him?

There were too many things left unaddressed. We had flown into this so unprepared, just like we had entered into every last thing we'd ever done. You can't just dig things up, I saw then. But then maybe you have to. We wanted to bring our old selves to the surface, that was part of it. We wanted to compare them to what we'd become. But I think now the broader goal, if we had one, was to see what it looked like when the sadness finally left you, finally let you rest. At this remove of years I can honestly tell you that I for one was not prepared for what we would find down there, whether Steven was a rotting hunk of meat or a gold-skinned angel in his heavenly repose. It wouldn't matter. He was out and away from us, and he'd escaped the thing that held us. He'd done it. Now the closest the rest of us could come was to dig up his corpse on a drunken August night in the shadow of the Jamboree and the Valu-Mart and Sarah's love and all the shit we'd torpedoed on our way to this sad, sick place, and no matter what we found down that hole or what we did with it, Steven would never be ours again. The lucky bastard.

EDWARDS, ON THE NEXT FLIGHT OUT OF TOWN

Edwards, wild, couldn't get out of the first. He put the first three guys on and then walked one in, gave up a double, followed by a hard single. Boom-boom-boom. Nothing was working. His curve had no bite, his heater no heat.

We brought in Reyes. He went 1-2-3 and made it look easy. Afterwards I saw Edwards in the tunnel and I think he was crying. He had been coming apart, we all saw it. This was exactly what he didn't need. He untucked his jersey and then threw a water cooler at the clubhouse guy.

On his phone later I heard him telling someone, I think his wife, that he should just come home. Leave the money on the table and catch the next flight, fuck this. You see a lot of guys buckle, but not usually so quickly, so completely. I felt for the guy. But I wanted his job. You're supposed to want his job. This isn't charity. So after all this I got a few starts and I did alright for us. Hit my spots, struck some guys out, kept the ball in the park. It raised my profile, got me traded to New York for prospects, got me into the play-offs. So when you think about it that way, I owe it to him. I owe this ring to Edwards.

I WAS A WILLOW

In the weeks after Ted Kane died I came to hate my own celebrity, as though having a dead boyfriend was the best thing I could have done for my own teenage popularity. I'd had Ted and then he exploded and left me with nothing but the pity and concern of a town full of strangers. All the boys and girls who'd never given me a passing glance were now suddenly offering a shoulder, a hug, an ear, a drink, a toke.

"All boys are fugitives," my mother once told me. She was full of rules and sayings and pearls of wisdom. I have none of these. I certainly don't have rules. Not with my girls. I have intent. I have vain prayer. "They're all fixing to go," she went on, "running from something, or to something else." What she neglected to mention was that some of them go up in the fireball of a modified M-80 before they ever get a chance to run away.

This was 1980, the year we moved into the house on Pine Glen Crescent. By some trick of seniority and luck my father had gotten off the line and into the offices of Springer Electric, and so we moved up a bracket. We traded in our east side rowhouse for a single family with attached garage on a quarter acre in a leafier, richer neigbourhood on the west side. The cars were bigger. The basketball nets in the parks were lovely and new. The boys even seemed taller.

We moved in July so by the time school started we had pretty much settled in. Of that summer I remember thunderstorms that would roll through Cavanagh like passing trains, two or three a night it seemed, leaving everything fat and ripe to the point of bursting: the impossibly green grass, the clean-feeling air in the morning. I remember my best friend Cassie Sherman's parents leaving for the Labour Day weekend, and I remember the party she had. I remember kissing Teddy there, being tickled by the moustache on his sweet face, and the smell of cigarette and pot smoke caught in the brown carpeting of his beige 1974 Dodge Tradesman van.

My memories of the explosion itself are a bit sketchier. This is probably my mind trying to protect itself from total insanity. What I hold onto is the November chill, and the stillness before the blast, then a rush of air from the other end of the culvert. Then the explosion, a noise like I have not heard since, everything going white, and then blue. Silence, and then a ringing, and then more echoes, water dripping. Then the recognition that Ted, who only an hour earlier had taken my precious flower, was gone.

The dusk was smoky pink the evening of Cassie's party. There were already fifteen or twenty people flopped around the yard and you sensed the neighbours were on high alert, waiting for their excuse to call the cops. But really, what more did they need? A house and a yard full of teenagers drinking beer, smoking, and soon crawling into every dark corner of the Sherman house to paw at one another.

We all went to Cavanagh District High and back then half the school was made up of those country boys that surround this town like a pack of wolves. Teddy, of course, was one of them. They'd drive their pickups and road rockets into town, roar through the lot like they owned the place. It was terrifying and unspeakably alluring to a girl like me. Cassie had a thing for country boys, too, the ones with crap on their boots and danger in their eyes. But then Cassie had a thing for all boys. She'd be the first to tell you that.

Ted Kane was quiet, though liked. Nobody had a problem with him, he just wasn't all that visible. He didn't crack wise, he didn't pick fights, and he didn't puff up his chest. He just *was*. Not a great student, and not a terrible one. Shy, not snobby. Unfashionable, but not an eyesore. He was a handsome boy, and I'd liked him since grade nine, I'd just never done anything about it. Now we were starting our last year of school, and I guess I was feeling a sense of urgency.

So Cassie and I filled balloons with water and tied them off. Ted was standing near the maple tree in the Shermans' front yard, in a circle with four other boys. They were talking, I remember, about who was going to sit at the top of the complicated social pyramid of CDHS. It was a pressing topic for all of us, because the Carmichael brothers were no more. Stevie Carmichael had ruled the school with daring and a pair of green eyes you just kind of wanted to jump into, but had graduated the summer before last, and Wayne, his younger brother and natural heir—who looked like a rat and was wired all wrong—was on his way to Joyceville for beating the life nearly out of somebody who'd looked at him sideways.

Ted was saying, "District's gonna be a lawless town," when I came up behind him, raised the red balloon above my head, and brought it down across the back of his neck and left shoulder, where it broke open and splashed, and

Teddy said, "Oh, shit!"

He turned and we wrestled. I was laughing. Teddy had my arms and Cassie was dancing around us and trying to get another balloon into my hands. Ted was laughing and saying, "You're gonna pay, Samantha Wallis, you are going to be so sorry."

And then we were on our way to his van, parked below a streetlight halfway down the block, where he was going to change his shirt. "Lucky for you I've got another," he said.

"How lucky for me."

As we stood next to the open side door of his van, the carpeted interior radiating an intense heat, he peeled off his wet shirt.

Ted's dad dug wells, and his mom worked for the school board. But both his uncles had dairy farms nearby, and that's where he worked summers. The result was that farm boy's body, those country muscles. Almost eighteen, skin kissed brown by the sun. I could picture him shirtless, holding a shovel, or at a swimming hole, or bending in to kiss me. I could picture him every time I closed my eyes. At the bottom of his ribcage the lines pointed toward his jutting hipbones that always peaked out above the top of his jeans; I never once saw him wear anything but jeans.

He dug a blue T-shirt out of the back of the van and pulled it over his head, then ran a hand through his hair. The image would be perfect in my memory were it not for that ungodly moustache.

I thought he would kiss me then. It just seemed like that kind of moment. But he didn't. He looked at me and smiled, then said, "Let's get back there and party!"

"Right on," I said.

It got cold that night, as though summer had just upped

and left. Darkness came all of a sudden, purple changing to black. Ted and I stuck close for most of the rest of the party, holding hands as we waded our way through groups of people doing all sorts of terrible things. I used to get those "If my mother could see me now" moments all the time, and I was having one then. I still get them.

We were in the kitchen, eating chips and sharing a can of Molson Ex, when Cassie came in looking unwell, wearing Adidas shorts and a jean jacket, her skin the colour of pond ice. With her bluish, cloudy eyes she gave me the thousand-yard stare and sat down stiffly in one of the chairs.

"Where have you been, honey," I said, "and what have you been doing?"

"I'm not really sure," she said, "Rodney Struthers, I think." At that we both laughed. But here's what's truly funny: seven years later, my first love dead and my prospects dim, I married Rodney Struthers.

Then Cassie's mind seemed to snap back into her head. Her eyes got clearer and she looked at Teddy and me. "How are you two?" she asked. The "you two" sounded significant in a way that sent something racing through my body.

"Decent," Ted said. I blushed.

"*Decent*," she mocked.

Rodney came into the kitchen. He said, "Hey," but looked down, like he was trying to avoid Cassie's eyes. We all said hey. His moustache was worse than Ted's.

Somebody was playing Aerosmith on Mr. Sherman's turntable, and it sounded like they'd blown his speakers. It was crowded and loud and annoying in the house. Teddy said, "Let's go hang out in the van," and each of the half-dozen people in the kitchen assumed he was talking to them, so we all went out together: me, Ted, Cassie, Rodney,

Missy Bell, and Jennifer Arcand.

Ted turned the radio on. Blondie played, then the Eagles. There were speakers in the back of the van, buried in the same carpeting that covered everything. Ted had an old orange recliner back there, and big, thick blankets that you could curl up in. There were no windows, but he told us he wanted to have those small bubble windows put in. His father had bought the van used from a television repair business and Ted helped him strip out the fixtures in the back. He had plans for the van beyond the windows. "A sweet paint job," he said, to cover up the beige, "and I'm gonna put a built in sofa bed, and, like, a bigger stereo. A little fridge over there, then maybe a TV."

"Sweet," said Rodney.

Ted lit a joint and we passed it around.

"I'll have it set up so I can live in it, if I need to," he said. I took a puff and handed the joint to Cassie. I wondered why he would need to live in his van, but decided it's just the kind of thing an almost-eighteen-year-old boy wants to imagine himself doing. Cassie took her drag, then handed the joint to Rodney.

"Here ya go, Rod," she said, kind of loudly, and then we all laughed for reasons I couldn't quite make out.

"Crazy on You" by Heart came on the radio then. "Everybody shut up," I said. "I want to hear this song. I love this song." But instead everybody started making fun of it, banshee wailing through the chorus. Everybody except Rodney, who just looked at his shoes.

When the joint was done, and the next one gone, too, Cassie sighed, "I guess I should check on the house, or whatever." She rose up on her knees, then turned and started fiddling with the door's handle. She said, "Is there a trick, or…" and then Ted reached over and popped it open. The cooling night air rushed in, and the cloud of smoke poured out. It was as though we'd forgotten there was a rest of the world to think about. Missy and Jen followed Cassie, and Rod just kind of disappeared, a trick he's still practicing.

There was suddenly a chance to be alone with Ted, and I tried to stay cool. He crouched in the open door of his van and said, "You want to, I don't know, hang out more?"

"Sure. Sounds okay."

He pulled the big sliding door shut and offered me a blanket. I thought that was so sweet and chaste. I didn't want to be chaste, in that moment. I wanted his mouth on mine. I wanted his hands. And yes, I know my daughters will soon want the same thing, and the little hell that'll put me through will be the only sort of justice we ever get, won't it?

But I didn't know how to get from where we were to where I wanted us to be, so I took the blanket and folded myself up in the recliner. He sat in his captain's chair, and we talked. He pulled the leftovers of a six-pack from beneath the dash and opened a can. "You want one?" he asked.

"I think I'm okay," I said. I was high and hungry, perched on the edge of something that, if I went any further and got tipped into, I'd have a hard time climbing out of.

We talked for an hour. It's hard now for me to remember ever being like that: open. Wanting to tell someone everything. I told him anything I could think of about myself and about my life, and then he leaned in and kissed me. I could feel it coming, could actually feel the downy little hairs of his moustache before his lips met mine. We locked together, and he held my shoulders. I didn't know what to do with my hands, so I put them on the back of his neck. We twisted our heads and he licked my front teeth, and then we pulled away and laughed.

"Finally," I said. "Christ."

He sighed. "You're amazing, you know that?"

"What are you even talking about?" I said.

"I look around," he said, "and I go, 'Everybody here is always gonna be stuck here. We're all gonna die in this friggin town.' But I look at you, and I see how somebody could be happy. Like, how I could be happy."

"Wow," I said, then put my head on his chest. "I'm so high right now. I feel so good."

Maybe he was nothing special, but he was nice to me and had dreams that didn't involve hurting people. He liked explosions, he said, and fireworks, not for what they destroyed, but for the energy they released, the mania of it.

In those moments after we kissed I let myself think of a future with Teddy Kane, when we weren't speaking, when we were just lacing our fingers together and breathing, feeling one another's warmth. I thought of a farmhouse outside of Cavanagh, and I thought of Ted in a plaid work coat and muddy boots. I dreamed of him coming home and stepping out of a truck and kissing me on the porch. Mostly I dreamed about us not being in Cavanagh.

I didn't dream of clipping coupons. I didn't dream of dumping a can of cream of mushroom soup into a pot of noodles, adding a can of tuna, and calling it a casserole. I didn't dream of finding that all the things my mother made look easy were anything but.

Ted and I didn't do much in his van that night. We just got closer and closer, and slower and slower. We weren't talking a lot. Our eyes were closed. I kissed him on the forehead and he started awake and said, "I'm glad you're still here."

He was exhausted, and completely wasted. His face was

red and his eyes were like slits. He said, "Keep me awake, Sam." So I sang to Heart to him:

> *I was a willow last night in your dream*
> *And I bent down over a clear running stream*
> *Sang you the songs that I heard up above*
> *And you kept me alive with your sweet flowing love*

I stretched the last note out, just like Ann Wilson, I swear. I used to be able to sing. Teddy turned and looked at me. His eyes were glassy and red. It was dark in there, just the streetlight glare coming in the windshield, but I could see that. "Jesus, Sammy," he said, "you're good."

"You have no idea, Teddy," I said, and at that moment I decided that I would one day take off my clothes for him.

Later—the next day, actually, once everyone was gone, once Ted and I had slept in the van until 5:00, and he'd woken with a start, walked me to the Shermans' front door, kissed me goodbye, and sped home in the hopes of getting there before his dad woke up, once there was just the aftermath and the cleanup to think about—Cassie and I sat beneath the patio umbrella and ate dill pickles right from the jar. I told her that I was in love with Ted. She said, "Whoa! Careful, honey!" It was just desire, she said, desire like a fog, blanking out everything. But it would soon burn off and be gone, Cassie told me.

I told her no. It wouldn't be like that.

Yes, Teddy, you are going to die in this fucking town. We all are.

I'm told there used to be a strict town-and-country divide at CDHS. There was one and there was the other, and that was that. I don't know who the first was, but once a country boy started dating a town girl it was like a crack in the dam, and by the time we arrived, a new flock of grade nines trembling in our boots, it was common practice. So Ted and I walking the halls on Monday, hand in hand, raised no eyebrows. Country boy, town girl. It was just another day.

We kissed outside classrooms. We held hands on the sidewalk out front, where everybody smoked their cigarettes. We ate lunch together. On weekends he'd pick me up in his van and we'd drive around, or park, or stop by Cassie's house. Slumped together beneath a heavy blanket, high, tired: that was the pose we held all autumn long. He got his hand up my shirt, nothing more. Cassie kept telling me, "You're going to lose that boy if you don't give it up." But Cassie, I learned, could be wrong about these things.

Finally, as November rolled in, the leaves almost gone, Teddy announced there'd be a party at his house. There was no reason for the party other than it had been a month or more since somebody had had a real good one. Mr. and Mrs. Kane were in Belleville with her sick sister, and they'd taken Bradley, Ted's little brother, too, leaving Teddy behind. So what we had was an empty house and some full bottles. We took it upon ourselves to reverse that ratio. It doesn't take many phone calls to round up a few dozen high school kids.

The usual crowd gathered and the usual things happened. The smokers hung out on the porch. There was the constant noise of trees on fall nights, the skiffing sound as dry leaves are blown across pavement. Behind Teddy's dad's workshop they were having wrestling matches. People coupled off and disappeared into bedrooms and closets. The heavy stoner kids took over the stereo. Cassie sat at the kitchen table with four other girls and regaled them with her complete sexual history. There was a lot of laughing.

Teddy took me by the hand. We were buzzed, but not out of our gourds. I think we both knew what was coming. We were both excited and we were both scared, but it felt inevitable and crucial. Like a thing we couldn't stop. I'm not sure what good caution would have done us, anyway, just like I'm not sure what good it's doing me now.

All the bedrooms were occupied, including his, so we went out to his van, which was parked under some trees alongside the house, and he started it up and ran the heat to take the chill off, and then we lay the blankets out and I undressed for him, on my knees, and he undressed, and we kissed, and then I lay down, and he was on top of me, and we did it. Just like that. It was both harder and easier than I expected it to be. It wasn't roses, but it wasn't all thorns, either. I was scared, but so was he, and his hands told me that he loved me.

After, we wrapped up in the blankets and lay there, and when the chill came back he started the van to get the heater running. I kissed him and smelled the sweaty, earthy scent of him, and the traces of dampness that I knew to be from the Kanes' old farmhouse. When somebody banged on the side of the van a while later we quickly dressed and then went back into the party one at a time, me first, as though it mattered to anyone what we'd been doing out there. We drank more beer and shared a joint and sang along when Bobby Culter and Danny Deeth got out their guitars and played "Heart of Gold" in the family room.

I lost Teddy for a while there. He drifted out of the room and I assumed he was taking care of something, or someone, but I think now he must have gone out to his dad's workshop. When he came back he had a green nylon backpack, and his plaid coat and big work boots on. He told me and a few other people there was going to be a light show outside. He had this big, beautiful smile on his face. I found my coat and shoes and he led me by the hand, outside, down the porch steps, and into the cold night.

He went across the lawn, which stretched out to the side and back of the house, and down a tractor path, muddy and rough. I was trying to keep up with him while jumping puddles, leaping from one grassy spot to another. It was cloudy and cold, but the night air was just barely lit up with that kind of pre-winter glowing. Teddy had a Maglite that he shone ahead of us. There were a bunch of people following us: some of the stoners, Cassie, Rodney. Mike Stronick was there, a kind of a popular kid, a big name, and he shouted "Hey, Kane, this better be good," in a way that made you know that Ted had moved up a rung on the social ladder by having the party.

The path led by the edge of one of the fields the Kanes leased out for hay, and then down a bank toward the road. There was a shallow stream there, and big metal culvert where it went under the road. Near the mouth of it Ted stopped and set his bag down. Everyone kind of congregated there, maybe fifteen kids. He zipped the bag open and handed another Maglite to Mike. He dug a handful of Roman candles out, about four or five of those little cardboard tubes, and he walked toward the stream and propped his own light on some rocks, pointing down into the culvert. Then he stepped into the stream. It was just a few inches deep, and he stepped carefully out into the middle of it, and farther into the dark metal tube, which was ten or twelve feet tall at its highest point.

With a plastic lighter he started lighting the Roman candles and holding them at his belt, letting the little fizzing balls pop out of the tube and shoot into the culvert. They looked beautiful, little balls of light rocketing through the air, flashing across the corrugated metal sides of the tunnel, throwing Ted's shadow everywhere. They made a wonderful noise in there, too, like *POPshewwwwww*. Cassie was standing on the bank, talking to Lisa Gooden, I remember.

I walked down to watch Ted. He lit another tube and they went *pop-pop*, and the little sparks landed in the film of water and died. Mike Stronick, holding his Maglite over his head like a floodlight, had come closer to watch, along with another boy named Phil Boyle. When that tube was done they stood talking a minute. Phil was smoking a cigarette. Then Ted walked out of the stream and over to me and he said, "How are you, Sammy?" and I said, "Good, Teddy." "Good," he said, and then, "I love you, Sammy." He put his arm around my waist and he kissed me, and smiled. Then he went over to the backpack once more, and he pulled out a cluster of three short, red cardboard tubes, wrapped together with masking tape, with smaller charges of some kind stuffed in the middle. A single wick stuck out of the side of one of the tubes.

He said to Mike Stronick, "I call this baby Big Mama." It was kind of sweet to see, because he was trying so hard to impress Mike.

"Right on," said Mike. Then Ted walked into the culvert. He bent down and switched off his light.

"Turn yours off, too, Stronick," he said, and Mike did. Then Ted stepped carefully again into the stream. He got his lighter out of his pocket and fiddled with it a bit. I didn't know what he was intending to do. He couldn't lay the package down, because of the water on the floor of the culvert. I think he was trying to time it so that he could throw it just before it went off and have it explode in the air. He stood there, like he was rehearsing it in his mind.

"Okay," he said. "It's gonna be loud!" We all cheered.

His back was to me. He was lighting the thing, and then he was just standing there, looking down. He laughed. I remember that. He laughed nervously. And then it went off.

In a moment, of course, I realized what had happened. I fell to my knees and bent over, holding my stomach. There was a smell of dampness and of the blast, smoky, and of something else, something rawer, wetter. Was that the smell of Ted's insides? I remember wondering that. Then, almost right away, there was so much going on, people running, people screaming. A police car arrived at the house at some point, and then an ambulance. I don't really know what happened next, the order of it. Cassie was holding me and Mike Stronick was crying, running into the culvert and back out, screaming. Somebody had to grab him and hold onto him.

My mother caught me crying once, about Ted. I don't know how long after he died, but long enough that she thought I shouldn't be crying about it anymore. And do you know what she said to me? She said, "At least you didn't have to watch him walk away."

There was a period, maybe a month or six weeks after Teddy's death, when I couldn't think of him without throwing up. I thought I might be pregnant, that my teenage beau's flesh and blood legacy might be growing inside of me. But it passed. There was no baby in there. There was only the rest of my life, growing problems like limbs. Illnesses and bad habits and fear.

He was gone, and all the boys left here seemed even more stupid and coarse in his absence. They'd run the hallways like hooligan kings and most of them must've known that they'd never get out of this town. Their dads didn't; why would they be different? The girls would marry them and have their babies. The boys would give the girls headaches and garages full of empties. They'd die still working on the line at Springer. This is the default relationship in this town. Unsmiling women and men who are always laughing loudly, sloppily.

Even my parents' relationship worked that way, more or less. Dad was decent enough, underneath it all, but he wasn't good for much around the house. My mother, a patient island of stability, held it all together. Her apparent strength is the thing I have spent my adult life trying to live up to. Alongside that I've tried to bury the pain of watching Ted Kane blow himself up in a drainage culvert while doing a stupid trick. I haven't really succeeded at either.

I gave myself time to try and believe that it would have been different with Ted. That he was different, and that his goodness and our love would make things better for us. But I guess everybody starts off believing that, don't they?

After the funeral, part of me thought I should just leave Cavanagh. I still wonder if I should have.

We used to look at our parents and laugh, but we laughed to keep from crying. Everything they did seemed so boring, so sad. We said it would be different for us. But I go on living it, and not changing it, because that's what I've always done. It blows like a hurricane right over me and I just hang on.

I'm aproned and ponytailed, with dry hands and crow's feet. I've seen better days, but I can't remember most of them. I have two daughters, just like my mother, but the similarities really end there. She didn't hide like I do. She didn't cry in front of her kids as often as I do. I don't know what we, as parents, are supposed to do with these weaknesses. Whether we're supposed to contain them and refuse to show them to our children, or if the backstage stuff will give them some comfort in knowing we're all kind of struggling, so it's okay for them to feel that way too. I can say that I started out thinking I'd be impenetrable, and I may even have had a few good years where I looked that way to them, but after a while I got too tired for the act, and just started letting the rough edges show. It made me feel very much that I was not my mother. It made me admire her more, but also to feel sad for what she must have felt, and what I did not know. For all the ways we don't know one another.

I think of how I felt those few times my mother allowed her cracks to show even the tiniest bit. The only time I ever saw her throw up, into a kidney-shaped steel bowl, while lying in a hospital bed. The maybe two or three times I saw her cry. The one time I saw her lose her temper with my father over money.

The girls don't listen to me and neither does their dad. I feel like we always listened to my mom, though she might remember it differently.

I look at myself in the mirror now and I wonder, How did these heavy, frowning eyebrows become the dominant feature of my face? I used to have a cute nose that people noticed. But then I think, Fair enough; I do disapprove. I'm tired and I disapprove.

I'd be lying if I told you that I don't find myself thinking of Ted, and of the end of Ted, about five or six nights a week. It always seems to be there, that night, and those hours leading up to it. As memories go it's not a pleasant one, but it's familiar and for that reason comfortable, in a way, if that makes sense. It's like somebody mean or unkind who I see everyday on my way to work, someone I don't know, but I'd still feel sadness if she wasn't there.

I'm thankful that the thoughts and dreams aren't always the same. That'd be maddening, I think. Instead they change and shift, like a hundred variations on the same theme. Sometimes I focus on what we did an hour before he lit that fuse, and try to tell myself they aren't connected. Sometimes I try to remember the scene after it went off. Other times I try to think about what it must have been like to be him. Did it hurt?

And yes, sometimes I like to imagine that he was thinking of me just before he went up. Maybe picturing me singing to him. It's stupid, I know. Poor Teddy, he wouldn't even have had time to think.

He missed all the hard stuff. It started soon after he died and it hasn't stopped since. I thought that if I bent to it, I could weather it like my mother did. But I've been bending to it for eleven years now. In Rodney, I married my own father: present, but not really. I married every boy this town has ever produced. I married the whole goddamn town of Cavanagh. And I don't know how much longer I can bend.

On hot nights I'll take a cold bottle of beer to bed, lay on top of the sheets and below the open window, and I'll read magazines until I finish that beer and fall asleep. I'll probably have the bed to myself. Most nights Rod doesn't make it any further than the couch. Some nights he does, though. Not often, but every now and then. He'll find me in the bedroom lying on top of the sheets with my magazine and my beer. He'll say something he considers tender. Then he'll undo his belt and take off his pants, and he'll just start in like I'm not even there, like I'm a mannequin. So I act like one. I let him do what he wants, mostly, which really isn't much. Rodney doesn't have a whole lot of imagination. It takes just a few minutes. I say some things, make a few sounds. But mostly I lie there with my eyes closed. I lie there and I bite my lip, and I try to think of when it felt good. I think of newness and excitement. I think of bending without breaking, but I also think of a time when I wanted to break, to be broken without bringing the entire world crashing down. I think of a beige van. Water balloons and cigarettes. I think of an exploding boy, and how, awful as it sounds, maybe I am thankful that he never had the chance to walk away.

DARK BLUE

Donnie's dark blue F-150, lifted, all kinds of chrome and extras. Your sneaker on the running board as you hauled yourself up, passenger side, a waft of cigarette and rum and cologne as you swung into the seat. Beneath a sunset the colour of week-old bruises Donnie was leaning over from the driver's seat, offering a hand, but you didn't take it. A gentleman, you thought, but laughed to yourself. There are no gentlemen here. You weren't old, but you were old enough to know that.

"The only thing worse than the town boys are the ones out there," your grammy once said, nodding toward the perfect Manitoulin darkness, but what were you supposed to do with that?

So you got in Donnie's dark blue F-150.

Everything was still ahead of you. You were fifteen and newly reckless. You were fifteen and hopeful. You were fifteen and you thought you were ready.

When you got in Donnie's truck your dad was still alive, your mom wasn't sick. You didn't have little Mitchell and an empty spot in your bed in the shape of Chris, the boy's father. You hadn't taken a string of awful and demeaning jobs, hadn't been kissed by your manager at Wendy's, hadn't yet thought, "Why not just this once?" over and over. You hadn't nearly succumbed to anaphylaxis after being stung by the wasp hiding inside your can of Mountain Dew. You hadn't shaved your head, or dyed your hair purple-black, or chopped it off with the kitchen shears while standing before the bathroom mirror, crying. You hadn't yet sat on the bathroom floor staring at the cabinet, wondering whether to open it or just go to bed and sleep for a week.

Donnie hadn't yet treated you to a twenty-minute monologue about his dark blue F-150, its custom features, about that fact that he'd had it specially ferried in, about the interior fabric they don't sell in Canada but which he managed to have imported from the States, while the scrubby ditches flew by in the headlights' sweep of the darkening September night. Donnie hadn't yet asked you what grade you were in because he forgot. Donnie hadn't yet said, "Mrs. Fillion? I had her!" He hadn't yet made you laugh with his imitation of her.

When you climbed into Donnie's truck he hadn't yet disarmed you with his low chuckle, the one that made him seem older and wiser even than his twenty-one years, his job and his stubble and his very own dark blue F-150.

You hadn't seen your boy in an oxygen tent. You hadn't seen the inside of an ambulance. You hadn't seen the inside of a bar. When you got in his truck you hadn't yet really seen the mess we all make of our lives.

"Give 'em enough rope," your grammy used to say.

When you put your Adidas on the running board and hoisted yourself up and into the passenger seat of Donnie's dark blue F-150 you hadn't yet been asked for a blowjob by your nursing school ethics instructor. You hadn't yet dropped out of nursing school. You had yet to drop out of the veterinary assistant program at Cambrian. You had yet to lose a cat named Shorty to liver failure, and another named Mischief to old age, and a black lab named Ben to your dad's carelessness with a GMC V-8 engine suspended from a block and tackle. You hadn't heard hogs at the slaughter from outside Chris's family's barn. You hadn't washed the blood out of a man's jeans. You hadn't scrubbed his fingernails.

When you got into Donnie's truck you hadn't yet dealt with the complications of he said versus she said, or didn't say, or what your best friend Karen would believe in the face of what Donnie was saying, how he described to his friends what had happened. You had yet to tell Karen, "He just misunderstood. I wasn't clear." No local women had yet called you awful things as you passed them in the aisle at the Foodland when you just came in to pick up some bread and yogurt.

When you stepped up into that truck, and swung that heavy dark blue door shut, and tucked your hair behind your ear, and said, "Hey," you hadn't yet been overcome by his cologne. You hadn't laughed when he said, "I frigging love this song," as "Since U Been Gone" came on the radio. You hadn't yet felt a bit bad afterwards when it seemed that he might have been serious. When you got in that truck you had not yet been driven out of Providence Bay and into the scrubby nowhere in-island, and down a logging road to a pretty spot he knew, where the last of the sunset would be amazing, and then the stars would be so bright. You hadn't yet sat in the deepening dark as the engine clicked and Donnie told you about his mother and how her family had owned the land upon which you sat but had to sell, so that was why he didn't feel bad about trespassing. You had never heard him say, "Nobody can tell me I shouldn't be here." You had not yet, before stepping into that truck, ever been kissed by a boy, let alone a man, though others, including Karen, found this impossible to believe.

You hadn't yet stared out his truck window and up into the place where the sun dying over Lake Huron met the descending dark, a meeting held in a line so perfect looking it appeared drawn onto the sky by a careful hand, and been surprised when Donnie leaned in to kiss your cheek and then your neck and then grabbed your arm. You hadn't yet thought, "Oh god, not this." You hadn't yet said, "Donnie, I don't think," and then let your voice trail. Then, "I don't think we should." Then, "No." You hadn't yet thought clearly to yourself that closing your eyes would likely make it pass more quickly. You hadn't yet surprised yourself by wishing that the radio had been on to give you something else to think about until he was done. You hadn't noted the stink of his breath and the small sound made by the truck's suspension. Donnie hadn't yet driven you home and touched your hair and kissed your cheek and said, "Thank you, thank you."

When you stepped up to the running board and swung yourself inside Donnie's dark blue F-150, you hadn't yet felt like an intruder in your own house. You had not yet sat at the round table in the darkened kitchen with a glass of milk, red in the weak light of the microwave's digital clock. You hadn't yet sat listening to the hard September wind blowing east across Huron and beating against the side of the house and then been startled when your grammy switched on the overhead light and, looking at you there, said, "You're fifteen years old. You've got nothing to cry about, girl."

CYCLES

He was a meek man, my father, but constant in all things. He owned and operated World Press & Tobacco, a two-aisle indoor newsstand and smoke counter that had every newspaper worth reading and many more that weren't. There were also thousands of magazines catering to every obscure habit, hobby, predilection, and desire. There was a single rack of postcards and a display cabinet of cigars and cigarillos, pipe tobacco, and rolling papers. He mostly spent his days perched on a stool at the counter listening to jazz LPs, the likes of Wardell Gray, Sonny Stitt, and Howard McGhee. Behind him was the rack of Player's and du Mauriers, Cravens, and Export A's. He opened at 7:00 AM to sell papers and cigarettes to the office workers, closed at 1:00 PM, came home, had his supper and slept a couple of hours. At four in the afternoon he returned to the store and stayed open until midnight. Six days a week, closed on Sundays. He did that for better than thirty years.

I hated him for those midnights. I hated him for the comfort he took in small things, the quietness and sobriety of his life, his friendlessness, his slump-shouldered posture. Mostly I hated him for the vision he represented of the life that I might inherit. I had somehow come to swallow the idea that I would one day eat the world whole, leave my footprints all over it, but my father's life suggested such things weren't likely. It both saddened and frightened me.

My father, Richard Hamelin, was hopelessly out of step in all things, including fashion, politics, music, books, and television. He was a thin, mousy man, sharp-angled and awkward, but his loyalty and steadfastness were obvious from his unchanging wardrobe: the worn-kneed corduroy pants and nubby polyester shirts, an ancient peacoat with missing buttons and fraying cuffs, and always the same grey vest with a black satin back. On his feet he wore moccasin-style suede shoes.

He opened the store in 1972 right after he married my mother, Helen Masters, and three years after earning his degree in English Lit from Ottawa U. Soon I came along, and twelve years after that my sister Amy was born. I have always assumed Amy was a mistake. Maybe we both were. Maybe the mistake was in their even having kids to begin with.

My father was not a sports fan, and I was not my father, or so I wanted desperately to believe, so I felt that giving myself over to football would distance me from him. Is there something more than opposite? Polar opposite? I reasoned that loving and playing football made me the polar opposite of my father. People would look at him and look at me and they'd say: No way are they related.

Without asking I moved into a room in the basement. I hunkered down, read bodybuilding magazines, watched wrestling and football videos. That was my life.

I had already defied my parents' expectations by transferring to the Technical High School. Tech was where you ended up once you had decided, or had had decided for you, that academic success was not in the cards. Tech was where your future mechanics and HVAC guys went. If you didn't graduate from Tech, you were probably headed to prison.

But the entire point for me was football. I left a school with no football team for one with a feared squad. In grade nine I made the juniors and wound up a tight end, blocking on running plays and flaring out for short passes. I was quick and I caught a few good balls. I was also introduced to special teams, which is like a crash course in brutality. There are few legal venues as perfect for the adolescent male to work out his bloodlust as special teams.

By the time I was ready for the senior team, late in the summer before grade 11, my father had yet to see me play a single game. Looking back, I still can't decide if that was because of his fear of physical things, of seeing his son exposed to such danger, or if it was more of his steadfastness, his quiet stubbornness, the same steady adherence to order and consistency that got him to the store each morning and kept him there until midnight.

I started at tight end that season and was told that, as a rookie on the senior team, that was kind of a big deal. One practice that fall we were running some plays on offence, working on blocking schemes, lined up against the D-line and linebackers, with live hitting. We had this guy named Joel who played outside linebacker. He had a pencil-line beard and ridiculous designs shaved into the sides of his head. We all hated him, but he was a quick, strong defender, so we kind of had to let it go. On one particular play during this practice I was pulling a stunt, crossing paths with the guard on my right, and Joel came inside and didn't see me coming over. He had his eyes fixed on the quarterback. I hit him three-quarters on and laid him out flat. There was a terrific popping sound, the very thing you hope to achieve when you strap on shoulder pads with the aim of using them as weapons instead of as protection. Joel was starry-eyed, breathless, and chastened.

Three of the coaches later went out of their way to congratulate me.

Upon my retelling, my father would ask, "Was that really necessary? It was a practice, after all." But in the expansive moments that followed the hit—moments wherein my skin felt like chain mail and my blood felt like rocket fuel—every part of me, physical and emotional, said: I want to do more of that.

I decided that strength was the key, and so within a week I was on my first cycle. It wasn't hard to find the stuff: half the O-line and most of the defence were using. It wasn't a secret among the players, but a shared understanding. There was a second-string running back whose older brother worked in one of those health supplement stores, and he had a connection to a guy selling the real stuff. That was our supply chain.

When I started bulking up but kept my speed, Coach Doherty, who handled the defensive side of things, noticed me and said, "Let's try this meathead at middle linebacker" (Doherty called everyone meathead, because he couldn't remember names). That was how I went from O to D, which is kind of like switching tribes. It was immediately obvious to everyone that I had found my place. I began to walk differently.

Football became a rite, our shared religious observance. We were our own gods. The cycles were communion biscuits. On game days we augmented them with greenies, just to make sure we were extra alert and open to the grace of utter fucking domination. Before pregame drills we had a ritual: we would put on our helmets and shoulder pads and we would hit the school's brick wall a few dozen times at full speed.

Hammer, they called me. There isn't much choice when your name is Jason Hamelin; there's little art in the practice of concocting nicknames for high school football team-mates. Our quarterback, for example, was a tall, composed kid named Anil Mukerji. I'll let you guess what we nick-named him. That we liked him and that he was a very good quarterback did not prevent us from having a lot of fun at his expense. One of our best receivers, a guy named Mike Dorn, dropped one pass all season, in our first game. One pass. Next practice someone called him Butterfingers. By the next game it had been shortened to Butter.

Botterill was our left end, captain of the defence. We called him Killbot. I think I came up with that. Peter Skenks, centre, anchor of the offensive line, we called The Skunk. Stefan Moreau was Moron; he went on to get a scholarship at Temple. Trent "Weiner" Sweeney was later a walk-on at Syracuse, which is where I'd wanted to go. For most of us other guys, though—Bowser, Digger-Dog, Mother Jones, Shoes, Cowpoke, Goggles, The Towel—this would prove to be the end of the line.

But we didn't know that then. Then all I knew was that I was playing middle linebacker, the lynchpin, the keystone, quarterback of our justifiably feared defence. I was still doing special teams, too. Kick coverage, where what you do is line up with the kicker, and as soon as he kicks the ball you run as fast as you can and hit anything that moves. The hope is that you get a chance to hit the guy who caught the ball.

We were a gang of marauders set loose upon a village, a war party, a scourge. Unexploded ordnance, maladjusted and murderous young men galloping at full speed toward another band of like-minded miscreants, boys with daddy issues to dwarf my own, hormones firing like malicious pistons. Special teams was a place to work out ugly things, unleash pent-up aggression, engage in serious headhunting. Scores were often settled. You could line a guy up before the snap and be fairly certain you'd get a chance to hit him with a thirty-yard head of steam behind you. Boys would break teeth, bones, occasionally rupture soft tissue. It was a strange, sanctioned form of bloodletting, and when it was over we were patted on our backs.

Some of those boys have gone on to do terrible things as men. I wonder if they might have skirted such ruin if they had been allowed to continue playing football.

The Tech High Senior Red Raiders had a reputation. We demanded fealty, determination, effort. I don't think the coaches even knew how serious we were. The head coach was Robert Broussard. We called him Bobby Brushcut. His real job was teaching. I had him for applied math, and even in the classroom he always wore his turf shoes and his Red Raiders windbreaker. Sometimes he'd even have a whistle dangling from his neck. Brushcut was a football coach first and a math teacher only by necessity. But during class I thought I detected some loyalty to the material, some genuine love for the concepts, and this disappointed me. On game days he'd go right on with the lesson, as though it was a normal day. It was all noise to me; I'd only be able to concentrate on football.

It makes sense to me now: being applauded for knocking

guys' heads off contributed to a sense of self-worth in a way that academics and family life did not. Home was all about humility, and as a seventeen-year-old humility is not really in your wheelhouse. You kind of want to believe that you're a deity. I felt that I had licence to kill an opponent, if the situation called for it, and that I would not be punished as a result, but celebrated.

I walked the halls as though I was already a legend. The cycles brought me from solid to ripply to huge, and people noticed. One day at home I walked out of the bathroom without a shirt on, just a pair of track pants, and I ran into my father in the hallway. He looked me up and down, sort of casually, as though he was trying to hide it. And what I saw in his eyes as he took me in was great discomfort, maybe even fear. I liked that. It told me I was becoming a person of my own invention.

We practised in the morning and again after school. The October mornings smelled metallic and earthy. The cold air cleaned out your nostrils. Some mornings the mud was still frozen in the shape of our cleat marks and prostrate bodies from the previous day's practice. As the day went on it would thaw out and get good and runny.

Our uniforms were never clean. The light grey pants always bore the marks of earlier games and practices. They were grass-stained, mud-smeared, often bloody, and poorly mended. Mud was good. It said you went flat-out. But blood was better. Blood was a badge.

In the locker room we listened to Metallica and N.W.A. at an ungodly volume. We hung rookies by their underwear on hooks in the showers and then urinated on them. We punched one another. Batiste, who was a defensive back, used to march around naked asking everyone, "Is it funny?!"

Then he'd answer the question himself. "It ain't funny." He'd get into your face and yell, "Motherfucker, it is NOT FUNNY!" I don't know what wasn't funny, exactly, but I think we all got the general idea. The general idea was don't fuck with Batiste.

When not on the field I was in the weight room, watching myself in the mirror. I ate dinner alone in my room, watching lifting videos. It was a lifestyle that left little room for extras. I never saw my parents.

We finished that year 9-1, the only blemish on our regular season record a squeaker against Confederation that we lost 7-6 when our kicker missed an extra point going against a crazy wind. Then we fell in the semis to St. Leo. That game was like a fight in a prison yard. The difference was a fourth-quarter safety, which is two very cheap points, if you're asking me. Their nose tackle fell on Anil in the end zone, the ball like a live grenade beneath his stomach. Final: 9-7.

That was a bitter pill to swallow. It became the taste of the cycles that long off season, the chalky little supplement tablets.

I was a massive beast. I was going to eat your son. I was going to cause him serious head trauma, simply because he had the misfortune of suiting up in another school's uniform. It could be anyone. That's what I was prepared to tell the assembled mourners: It was nothing personal.

The next year was another matter. We rolled through that season like a thing sent to destroy young men, belongings, pride.

One quick thing I feel it's important to mention here: you always hear that one of the side effects is impotence, but I didn't see any of that then. I had no trouble, and no shortage of opportunity. If you can imagine the kind of girls who might attend a last-chance school like Tech, and who might then be attracted to boys like us, well, I knew the company of a good many of those girls.

It's true that the cycles proved a tough habit to break, as did the greenies. I think they left me kind of open to additional, let's say, weaknesses, too: cross-tops, oxy, sometimes red birds. I'm not saying no to any drinks, either. I don't work out much anymore, so I'm smaller, and certain parts of me are shrivelled and unsightly. My luck with women has more or less evaporated. That's all true. But it's important to recognize just how momentous a time in my life this was. For two years I was feared, adored, discussed. Other teams watched videos that isolated me and my actions. They concocted strategies to combat my skill and strength. They modified their game plans.

Every single girl I passed in the hall knew my name. How many people can say that about any part of their life? So, as shitty as things have been since—and they have been extremely shitty—I'm still tempted to say that, on balance, it was all worth it.

We were perfect, unbeaten. We had our revenge on St. Leo in the semis, 24-8, in a snowstorm. That was fun. It put us on a collision course with the City West champs, Brookside.

The championship game, called the Capital Bowl, was always played on a Sunday, so here was my father's chance to come and watch me play. Once we'd earned our berth I said to him, "Think you'll make it to watch the final?"

And he said, "Oh, now, I suppose that's possible."

That's possible. I wanted to say to him, "I'm your son!"

What I did say was, "It'd be cool if you could."

"I think I'm fighting a cold, Jason. It might be better for

me to stay home and get some rest."

I did not sleep the night before the game. Not one wink.

They held the Capitol Bowl at a neutral site, an Astroturf field behind a sports and rec complex with metal bleachers and a digital scoreboard. No change rooms, so we got into our pads and uniforms at Tech and then boarded the bus. As we got off the bus and sprinted out onto the bright green surface to begin warm ups I felt it under my feet: it was like a sheet of plastic laid down over a parking lot. I was looking forward to picking up some good citizen's son and body-slamming him down onto it.

Mom came, and she brought Amy. They sat halfway up the bleachers and they looked like they were trying to hide from the noise. They got cold and left before half-time.

During the pregames Boterill said to me, "Hammer, today I'm going to kill someone."

I said, "Yes you are, Killbot! My goal is to make these guys shit out their own teeth."

"Yes, guy!" shouted Killbot.

Brushcut called us in, had us all take a knee. After the usual niceties he began screaming at us: "Who are you going to hit?" and we were shouting back, "Everyone!" And then he asked us again, and we shouted louder, "Everyone!" The third time he asked, every member of the Tech H.S. Senior Red Raiders football team shouted louder than they had ever shouted before, barking "EVERYONE!" up into the clear November sky. But not me. I called out: "Richard Hamelin!" It was one of those things you do without fully realizing that you're doing it.

We kicked off to start the game. We swept down the field like a gale, like a hurricane, knocking over everything we encountered. You could have parked a garbage truck at midfield, and we'd have knocked that over. A yacht.

The wind was at our backs, which felt like the natural world confirming our dominance. Brookside's kick returner was tiny, and though that usually means quick, I caught him splitting between two blockers and I plugged the hole with my head. I was a giant arrow with a helmet at its tip. There was a target painted garishly on his chest, six inches below his chin, and once I was airborne I was not to be denied it. I was later told that I drove the poor boy back five yards, in the air. He did well to make it to the sidelines under his own power, though he did not return to the game.

We referred to that as "setting the tone."

Brookside's bread and butter was their running game. They had a battering ram of a fullback, a young man built like a truck, so the game promised plenty of hitting, lots of inside stuff. It was going to be a good day. Our defence took the field boisterously, wearing T-shirts beneath our pads that read TECH HS D-FENCE: YOU ONLY GET 2 CHANCES. This was Canadian football, remember: three downs. We were proud of that.

The Brookside offence tried to appear upbeat, but beneath it all they seemed stoic, maybe resigned to their unenviable fate.

The first play of the game was a run off tackle, to my left. We swarmed their little back like pack animals. There was soon a solid blanket of red over top of him. He might have managed a yard before we buried him, a kid with hopes and dreams smothered beneath an avalanche of acne-dotted flesh.

They went two-and-out. I was fatherless. I was adrift in a sea of pain. My consolation would come from spreading that pain to others.

The cycles made rage seem like the natural response to just about anything. Later in the first half Brookside pounded down to within field goal range. Every small advance felt like an insult, a tiny wound inflicted. I looked around, down the bench: what was wrong with us?

We stanched the bleeding, barely, and prevented them from reaching the end zone. Then their kicker put a wounded duck through the uprights: 3-0 Blues.

I did not take that well. I sprinted to the sideline, passing our kick return team on the way. I yelled at each of them, "Revenge! Revenge!" Once on the sideline I took my helmet off, crouched and, gripping it by the facemask, slammed it against the ground in an S.O.S. rhythm, clustered beats of three, then a pause, then three more. My cadence had a basis: I was tapping out WHERE'S! MY! DAD!, though I was conscious that it could also be heard as STOP! BROOK! SIDE!

On a play shortly before half-time their offensive line dropped back in pass protection. I hung back trying to eliminate any short little passes into the middle of the field. To my right I saw Joel give their tight end a nifty little swim move and race around on a clear path to their quarterback. But at the last possible second that fullback of theirs came over to give Joel a little shove, then fall, and add a highly illegal leg-whip that caught Joel in the thigh and knocked him down. At that same moment the quarterback moved up into the pocket a couple of steps and launched a rocket down field. It was a beautiful, tightly spiralling pass, a bullet, and it settled into the receiver's arms like a sleeping baby. He never had to break stride. Our safety pushed him out of bounds, but it was a thirty-odd yard gain.

The Blues offence jogged by us on their way to the new line of scrimmage, high fives all around. "Nice pass,

Matty," they were all saying to their passer, Jason Priestly in white high-top cleats.

I was offended. I wanted to injure him. I wanted to humiliate him, to make him question his abilities and choices. I wanted to hit him in such a way that he would quit football and one day open a small newsstand that sold stale old cigars and then have a son who would not believe in him.

That drive wound up netting them another field goal. On their next possession a couple of penalties and a botched running play put them back on their own 11 yard-line. On a second-and-long they ran play-action. Matty feigned putting the ball in their big fullback's arms, then pulled it back. I stood rooted to my spot in the middle, making him feel like he'd frozen me with his fake, but when he moved his eyes toward the sideline I broke right for him, a seam suddenly open in the line. I made for him with frightening abandon.

The hit was concussive, by which I mean not only that it knocked Matty onto his back, but that I believe the earth buckled a bit beneath the force of it. The ball dribbled out, away from the human pile-up, and toward Brookside's end. I heard voices rise behind me. I saw the eyes of their fullback, who was on the ground nearby, grow large with panic. Scrambling on my elbows and my belly, I chased the thing, grunting like a bush pig. I could feel bodies moving in behind me, but I got there first. I fell on the ball and it felt like a stone beneath my gut. As I rolled over and cast my eyes skyward I saw the zebra raise his arms, his pale hands stretching up into the cold sky to signal the touchdown. In the next moment I was at the bottom of a heap of Red Raiders, because that was how we celebrated: we attempted to drive one another into the ground.

Behind us, Matty writhed on the ground, gasping, unable

to catch his wind. I looked back there and I saw him experiencing his wordless pain, compounded by my touchdown, and I wished for that to be the image I took forward into my life after all of this. Not the later sight of Butter hauling in two TD passes to give us the 21-6 victory, not Anil hoisting the trophy, not Brushcut with tears in his eyes. Just that: Brookside's quarterback lying on his back on the shining green turf, alone, twisting into and away from the pain, fighting for his breath. That's what I wanted.

What I got was something altogether different. Now, the thing I remember most vividly—the single moment that seems most real to me all these years later—came a few days before I was told I would not be eligible to play in my final year at Tech, and that I would therefore, in all likelihood, never play in university. It came before nine other guys heard the same news. It happened several days after the Capital Bowl, on a skyless afternoon when I came home to find a police car in the driveway and an officer named Hurley sitting at the kitchen table with my parents, explaining that the head of our supply chain had been apprehended, and that the rest of the dominoes were now falling. We had all been named.

That was an excruciating conversation, but the moment I have carried forward like a cursed memento came late in the night after Officer Hurley's visit, in the wan light of the range hood's 40-watt bulb, as my father sat slumping over the kitchen table.

"Jason, I'm sorry," he said.

"Whatever, dad."

"Jason, you didn't do this alone."

"Sure I did," I said. "I make my own decisions, thanks."

"Jason, please, listen," he continued, "I've done what I

could for this family, but I see now that there are things I've neglected."

"Nobody cares," I said. "Nobody cares, Dick."

I know now that when my dad looked at me he saw a scared and broken boy, not a muscled man-beast overflowing with confidence and power and, in that moment, beset by injustice, which is how I'd sized up the situation. But though he'd been given every opportunity and excuse to revile me, it wasn't revulsion in his eyes; it was love, and sorrow, and regret. I couldn't understand that at the time, of course. I was full of a cloudy desire to make meaty pulp of other boys my own age, surrogate victims in helmets and contrasting jerseys. I'm certain those things, those rages borne of circumstance, biology, and chemistry are what made me say next, "Just fuck off, Richard."

I turned to leave the brown and orange kitchen, the curling linoleum, and the scrawny bullseye of my confusion and hatred, but he stopped me. He stood and he puffed himself up, though he was by then a good four or five inches shorter than me, and who knows how many pounds lighter. I recognized in his eyes then the anger that I had attempted to make my own nature, my bedmate, my goal and my consolation. He raised his right hand over his shoulder and he aimed to bring it across my face. But he just stood there, his hand held aloft, shaking a bit, the veins in his temples throbbing. And he never brought his hand down, he never hit me, whether out of fear or pity I did not then know.

I CANNOT BELIEVE WE ARE
HAVING THIS CONVERSATION

My stomach spills over my belt and folds my underwear at the waistband, and in general I don't much look like the guy I was when I played junior. I know that. Also my wife thinks I hit on the babysitter too much, but truthfully I'm saying the same things I always have, they just sounded different coming from the younger me.

"You call her sweetheart," Irina said.

"I call everybody sweetheart," I said.

"She is young and tiny and blonde with tight shirt and little shorts and you call her sweetheart. I think this is wrong." She tucked her pretty chin into her chest with her arms wrapped around herself.

"Irina, sweetheart," I said, then realized what I had said. "See? Right there! I didn't even know I was saying it!"

"I am your wife, you are supposed to be calling me sweetheart!"

I was so damn tired, you know, working fourteen-hour days selling cars. I didn't need this. The dog was barking at something, squirrels, birds, geese, whatever. Jaxon was wailing. He always cries. Two and a half, he's a crier. And his sister was throwing a fit because we were paying attention to each other and not to her. Anna's kind of like her mom in that way. They also look so much alike, they could be twins. They both look like they're made of glass, just so perfect.

"Everybody, EVERYBODY," I shouted, just to clear the air, just to shut everybody up for a minute. There was a split second of silence and I jumped in and said, "I am tired. Like, bone-tired. I just need, what I need is for everybody to settle down."

"Always tired," Irina said.

"Somebody has to sell those Hyundais," I said. "They won't sell themselves, you know. I mean, they could. If there was a car that could sell itself, that's it. But then I wouldn't get paid." At that moment the dog started up again, and that dog, Finnegan, he has the worst bark imaginable. Like a car horn in an aluminum shed, over and over and over.

"But you are doing too much," she said, and at the same time Anna, who's six, was yelling, "Dad Dad Dad Dad Dad," for no reason.

"I cannot believe," I said. "Why am I hearing this? Do you like your house? Do you like your clothes?"

Wolters, who works with me, Mike Wolters, he's what you might call my closest friend, we talk about everything. He played, too, got looked at pretty seriously by the scouts—Leafs, Flames, he says, and I think maybe Islanders—but then he wrecked his knee. That old story. But Wolters is a good salesman, almost as good as me, and we talk a lot. There are a lot of hours to kill when you're waiting for customers in January during a snowstorm and the economy is down. Wolters thinks I'm crazy to want this, to have married Irina and the kids and the house and soccer practice, the whole bit. Wolters likes his freedom. He likes screwing his way through the receptionists and the single moms who come around looking to trade in their exes' performance cars. But I tell him, there's nothing like looking at your kids while they sleep, or staying up late with the woman you love to wrap their Christmas presents.

And Wolters hears that, and he nods his head, way up there on his massive shoulders—Wolters has six or eight inches on me—like he gets it, but I know he doesn't get it. He's happy to know I'm happy. But then he's looking at me, I know this, and he sees my gut and how I'm kind of soft and how I'm standing on the sidelines of my kids' soccer games while he's at a core class at Goodlife, planking and sweating, his face not two feet from some girl's amazing ass in those yoga pants and when the class is over he'll have her number and the next day he's at his desk getting pornographic texts from her while Irina's calling me because Jaxon threw up on her cashmere.

When this all happened, the four of us were in the dining room trying to have a nice Saturday morning, and I had been trying to get through the sports section on my iPad, just relaxing with some hazelnut coffee from the Keurig. I had mentioned to Irina about seeing the Avengers movie, and said maybe we could get Leanna to come and watch the kids and put them to bed on Thursday, when Irina kind of blew up about it, saying all that about sweetheart. At the same time, Jaxon had just kind of drifted away from the table to dump a box of toy cars all over the place, his hands and his face still all sticky from juice and cereal. And Anna, when her mom and I started talking, wanted the iPad so she could play games. I think that's why she was saying "Dad Dad Dad" over and over.

"Irina, honey," I said, "I don't know what it's like in Russia, like when you were younger, but here we can use names like sweetheart and not have it be like a blood feud between crime families or something." That she did not like.

"I cannot believe the things you say," she said.

"Well, I say them," I said. "And about the other thing, this life you have, that we have and we love, and all the things we use and like, they need me to sell cars. So I put on a tie and go to the dealership and I sell cars, and I bring things home to you. That's how it works. That's how it's always worked."

Irina, really, I think sometimes she's still upset about how things started. She still says, if you ask her, that I misrepresented myself before we met, on the form she got with all the information about me and where she'd be going. It said OCCUPATION: and I wrote HOCKEY PLAYER, which she took to mean professional hockey player, even though by then I had not been drafted and had exhausted my junior eligibility and given up, more or less, on the big dream. But to defend myself, since it said OCCUPATION, I figured, well, it doesn't say JOB, it says OCCUPATION, and I was still very occupied with the idea of being a hockey player. I was playing three nights a week in two leagues, one with the guys from the dealership, including Wolters, who had been really, really close to the big leagues, and so the skill level was obviously there. Plus, if you've ever been around these things, you know that a lot of deals get made before, during, and after the games, so professional wouldn't really be stretching it. And besides, I never wrote PROFESSIONAL HOCKEY PLAYER. I wouldn't do that, because it wasn't true.

"All the time, it's just me and your kids," Irina said.

"Baby."

"Yes?"

"They're your kids, too."

This whole time, oh my God, the dog would not stop barking. Somebody should have told me about Shelties before I let Irina go and buy one. I mean, holy, barking all the time.

And on top of this, Jaxon was getting antsy. Anna was good, because I slid her the iPad during all this, knowing I wasn't going to be able to finish the sports section, so she was playing something on there. But Jaxon had already dumped out that bin of cars—dinky cars, we used to call them, but they probably don't call them that now—and then moved back to the wall unit, to the lower cubbyholes where the toys and games are, and he was pulling out this giant floor puzzle and I could see he was about to dump that out all over the place.

"One thing at a time," I said to him, as per the rule we had written on the fridge on a blue piece of paper that the kids decorated with stickers. The rule was in place, really, to make it so Irina and I would have fewer toys to pick up at the end of the day, because on Monday mornings I really did not need to hear about how the cleaning lady had complained to Irina and made her feel terrible for being so lucky for marrying a man with a good job and a big house and having bratty kids with too many toys they never pick up. I mean, can you imagine saying this? To somebody who is basically your boss?

But Jaxon dumped the puzzle, not listening to me, so I stood up, maybe pushing my chair back a little too hard, because it bumped the sideboard and made Irina say, "Hey!" and got Anna to look up from the iPad and say, "Daddy?" Then Irina said something quietly to Anna in Russian because she's been teaching her some things I don't understand, and that kind of bugs me, them being able to talk without me understanding it.

"Sorry, what was that?" I said.

"I just said that here you go. 'Here goes Daddy,' I said."
"Meaning what?"
"Meaning that here you go to take care of things."
"And so?" I said.
"And so take care of it!" Irina screamed, and it really made me step back. I wanted to know what was going on there, but I had to handle Jaxon. I went over to him and he was looking at the puzzle and trying to pretend I wasn't there. "Jaxon," I said, "did you hear me? I said one toy only. You have to tidy something up before you get the next thing. Remember the rule sheet?"

But he just kept looking down, and when I went down on my knees, which isn't the easiest thing for me actually, but I did that to look him in the eye and he gave me the smile he gives when he knows he's doing something wrong but for him it's a joke. That sets my brain on fire.

"Jaxon?" I said. "Jaxon, you are not listening to me. I'm your father. Why are you not listening to your father?"

He didn't say anything. Ignoring me is my button. It's going to set me off every last time. You have to know this about me.

The dog was still barking. I was standing ankle-deep in big cardboard pieces of puzzle and dinky cars and Jaxon was completely ignoring me.

"You do not ignore me!" I said, with my lowest bass voice, my scariest one, the one that the kids hear and they know, okay, that's trouble. "Don't you ever ignore your own father!"

Irina put her hands over Anna's ears for reasons that were lost on me. My face felt hot all of a sudden and my mind was like gravy, but I knew enough to think to myself, "Why is she covering Anna's ears?"

"Don't be his bully," Irina said.

"His bully?" I said. "I'm his father. I cannot believe this. Why are you talking like this?" My heart was thumping and the dog was barking, but I did my old trick where I make it quieter in my mind. It was like being in another team's barn again, the first time I'd felt that way in years, like all my muscles were ready for whatever happened and I could block out all the distraction and just focus in. Tunnel vision. I forgot about my stomach and the waistband of my boxer-briefs, the way it was folded over. I forgot that I usually wear a really tight undershirt or those compression top things under my suit. It was like jumping back in time. It was like I was wearing skates and pads.

I could hear Irina getting shrill, now she was shrieking at the dog, "Shut up, stupid Finnegan. Shut that dog up, shut it up, shut it up!"

But I was focusing on the Jaxon problem. I did a thing I do where I pick him up by the ankles, so he's upside down, and I haul him way up so I can look him in the eyes, upside down, his feet way over my head. He mostly likes it but Irina freaks out. Sometimes he laughs and wiggles around, but if I do it quickly, and I have on my really angry face, it upsets him and I can use it to get a point across.

"Jaxon," I said, holding him up there, "are you going to listen to your father?" And he was looking at me, and his bottom lip was starting to go right before the tears, and his eyes were squinting, and he was all red. I felt like it was working, like I was getting my point across but just then Irina let go of Anna's ears and came racing over to me at a million miles an hour and was trying to get Jaxon from me, yelling at me, stepping on my foot.

She said, "Awful! You are awful! Why don't you let us be and then you can fuck that babysitter?"

I said, "Okay, what? Wait, wait, wait. First of all, language, honey." I put Jaxon down on the sofa then, just swung him down, and he was upset, he put his face in his arms, poor guy, all that commotion. Anna started crying back over there at the dining room table. I said, reasonably now, snapping back out of that hockey frame of mind, back to being a calm husband and dad, "Irina, get it under control. You look like a wild woman. You look terrible. Where's pretty Irina?" I said, "Where's the pretty girl I married? You need to be pretty." I tried to get a pause, and a deep breath, then a smile. The smile would mean we were out of the woods. "Right?" I said. "It's why I keep you around."

It was one of those things where, again, you know, these are all things I used to say, and people would love me for it. Women, girls, their mothers. It's like Wolters and I were talking about once, about how if you're tall and cut and have nice clothes and you follow a girl around, it's romantic, but if you're ugly and poor? Then you're creepy. You're a stalker.

Irina was quiet for a moment. She caught her breath, but there was no smile. The dog was growling, but not barking, and I could hear his claws skittering across the ceramic tile in the kitchen, coming closer to us. Anna cried in the back of her throat, but quietly. It was sort of still for a moment. I was breathing heavy, in through my nose, out through my mouth, in through my nose, out through my mouth. Jaxon broke the quiet. He rolled over on the couch and he was looking up at us standing there.

Then, for reasons I just can't even, like I don't even know, he started saying, "Shit on your head, shit on your head, shit on your head," and I don't even know where he learned that. Who would say that?

I looked at Irina with this confused look on my face, and

I said, "Where in the hell would he learn something like that?" and Irina went right into attack mode, screaming at me, "What does that mean? Are you saying I am bad mother that I teach him these bad things?" and just losing it. When you get somebody where it hurts most, you know, they tell you that with how they react.

Finnegan, he came over now and he was bouncing around our legs and barking again like crazy, nipping at my pant legs. I gave him a little kick and he came right back, barking, nipping.

"You say I am bad mother," Irina said, "but what other woman would be mother of your kids?"

I said, "What? Come on!"

Irina said, "Oh, shit on your head, shit on all your heads! I did not come here for this!"

Then I said to her and to Jaxon, to both of them, because it is another one of our rules, I said, "Bathroom words stay in the bathroom."

"I know rules!" she wailed. Like, I have never heard her scream like that.

The dog, he was barking louder, I couldn't believe it. I thought the neighbours would, you know, like maybe we could expect the cops to ring the doorbell any minute. I wanted everyone to quiet down, I thought being quiet and sitting down and taking deep breaths would be useful, would change the feeling in the room enough that we could make ourselves understood.

"Shit on your head, shit on your head, shit on your head," said Jaxon.

"We need to calm down, everybody here," I said, but the dog kept barking and Anna kept sobbing, and Irina was making fists and pushing my chest with them. She said, "I have had enough of this." Which was worrying to me, it told me she was trying to check out of the conversation. So I went down to the front door, and Finnegan followed me like I guessed he would, because I think he saw me as the aggressor in everything that was happening, so I opened the front door and I pushed him outside with my foot and then I slammed the door and I watched out the little window. He just stood there for a minute, tilting his head, but then he saw something, like a bird or a squirrel, and he bolted. Right out across the street—I watched to make sure he didn't get hit by a car—and then through a couple of front yards, right over the Maxwells' flowerbed, and around the corner, gone, like he couldn't wait to get away from us. Who could blame him, I guess. All that screaming.

The kids freaked and ran to the front window to look for Finnegan, but Finnegan was totally gone by then. And Irina got real quiet, didn't even try to comfort the kids, she just came over and got right into my face, and she said, "You are awful. You don't have a heart. I hate this! And I hate you!"

"Irina," I said, "you be careful." I said, "You know I could still send you back." And I regretted that right away, if I can be honest with you. Her face just turned to stone. I guess it was hard to hear what I'd said, and I wasn't even sure it was true. But it felt true. I felt very angry and truly powerful, and like I could do anything I wanted. There were hot tears running down her cheeks and chin and her neck. Right down into her blouse. And I took a breath and I looked at her. The redness cleared from in front of my eyes, it was like clouds blowing away and then a big blue sky, and I could see her clearly. It made me happy and sort of sad at the same time. She was so beautiful. Thin and made-up and delicate. So pretty and lacy. She had worked hard to keep herself that way for me. She was still, I could see then, the same beautiful girl I saw eight years ago, the same girl I had picked from the pages of that catalogue.

"Asshole," she said, and then, in another one of those moments where if I had it back, you know, but I couldn't help myself, I went back to the front door and I opened it, and I said to Irina, "Why don't you run away, too, like the dog? See how far you get?" But that was crazy, and I knew it. I mean, where would she go?

"I cannot believe I came here for this," she said, then went upstairs and shut our bedroom door.

"Well, you did!" I called after her.

The rest of that day I was Public Enemy Number One, and nobody said much to me. I said to them, I get it: the dog. Okay. But you can't undo things.

That was a rough night, too, I'll admit. All I got was a good look at Irina's back. But in the morning, I said okay, let's go find Finnegan. And everybody cheered, and I felt good in the way a man does when he is happy with his decisions. We all felt the hope of a new day. My wife and my children sitting comfortably in our beautiful and roomy Santa Fe on a Sunday morning, me at the wheel, my driving gloves so snug and soft. Jaxon and Anna had so much hope in their eyes. We were united in purpose, all for one. How many times like that do you really get in this life? I'd like to know that. Everyone's tears had dried because they finally saw me for the compassionate man that I am, and together we shared a mission: we would drive the streets as a family, back and forth, around and around, and we would search and search, and we would find that damned dog, or we would fail trying.

THE RATE AT WHICH HE FELL

The third company I called said they could have a guy there that afternoon. The other two would have me waiting until the end of the week, and I've always felt like if you want my money, in this case thousands of dollars of it, you'd better jump through hoops, like being there the day I call, no matter what you've got on your plate.

"I can have my guy there this afternoon, if you're gonna be home," the receptionist said when I called Anderson Roofing Contractors.

"Yes, great," I said. "I'll be here all day. I work shift, so."

"Great," she chimed.

Three days earlier I had been up in the attic digging around for evidence of mice, which I was sure I wouldn't find. We'd been lying in bed reading a few nights before that when we heard a scratching-scuffling noise that Ellie said was mice in the attic. I felt no, it was squirrels in the gutters. But she said, "You'd better check that out." Ellie doesn't crawl into tight spaces. She doesn't do attics. So up I went and I didn't find any mice, which was a nice sort of vindication, but I did find dampness on the underside of the plywood up there, which had me feeling sick about the cost of a new roof. Later I climbed up on the roof to have a closer look, and sure enough, the shingles looked like hell. Throating: that's what they call it, I've since learned, when the little gaps between the shingle tabs start to wear away and get wider, and that's where the water finds the wood. We had plenty of throating. I climbed down and told Ellie about it, and she said, "What'll that cost?"

I dread these adult decisions, avoid them when possible and download them onto Ellie when there's a chance I can do so without being overly obvious. Minor adult decisions, like whether or not to tuck your shirt into your jeans, I can sort of handle. But then there are giant ones, like do I spend $7000 on a new roof, and where do I get that $7000? In our household, most of the big decisions require several rounds of negotiation. Ellie and I usually each advocate for one side, and we bring our best arguments to the kitchen table where we sit over coffee or beers, and we have at it, in a civilized fashion. Like our decision to name our son Jordan, which I sort of regret now. There are two other Jordans in his senior kindergarten class, and one of them's a girl. But Ellie lobbied hard for Jordan, and she came to the table with notes, research, a well-considered argument. I wanted something simpler, easier on the tongue, like John or Will or Billy. But I lost that one. I should have been better prepared.

This one about the roof I sort of won, if you can call shelling out several grand to a tradesperson a victory of any sort. What's the word for that? Pyrrhic. But in the end she said, "I guess you'd better call someone." That meant the roofing file was now squarely in my lap, and mine alone. I dug out the phone book.

But it wasn't until three days later that I finally picked up the phone. I shouldn't have waited even those few days; it was November. Anything that was going to be done would have to be done soon. But I was walking around the house in a funk as though nothing had been decided. Ellie would ask me at dinner, "Call anybody yet?" I'd say no, I hadn't, I was thinking. But I wasn't thinking, I was delaying, and by not pushing the matter she was complicit. That's us: we never finish the job. We might sort the laundry and get it in the washer and then move it to the dryer, load after load, and we might even get it folded, but it'll sit there, folded in baskets in the middle of the living room floor for days.

So finally I called. The first two places, the outfits with the biggest ads, wanted me to wait a few more days, but Anderson—ARC said the ad in big letters, and then underneath in smaller ones NDERSON OOFING ONTRACTORS—said they'd have their guy out that afternoon. So I waited.

A blue truck pulled up. I was sitting at the kitchen table after lunch and I could see right through the living room and out the front window to the street. The truck was an F-350 with a cap and the letters ARC on the door. All I could see inside was the silhouette of a man in the driver's seat hunched over something. Papers, I imagined, or maybe a Blackberry or phone. He took his time getting out. I considered putting on my boots and meeting him out front, but then I thought no, just wait for him to ring the bell. Ellie was upstairs with Jordan. I think they were building something with blocks. Jordan's four and he likes to build roads with wooden blocks—just long strings of them laid out on the floor—but he says he needs help. Help amounts to you putting a few blocks down in the same sequence he's established, and then him saying, "Not there!" Ellie's got more patience for it than I do. She'll play along, ask him for the parameters of the situation, which are always shifting, whereas I'll usually just say, "Fine, you don't want help, be my guest, I'll be downstairs." Ellie sees the parental role as something like a shepherd: protect and point the way, always with extreme patience. I'm more like a traffic cop.

Finally the bell rang and I opened the door to find a walking handshake standing there, a bristly head and shiny dark eyes with a big, practised smile. "Mr. Mazurek?" he asked. "Yes," I said, returning the handshake and the smile. He said, "Name's Terry Locks," and he put a business card in my hand. It confirmed his name. So he wasn't lying about that.

"Call me Nick, Terry," I said, and then I put on my boots and moved outside to join him on the lawn. We stood beneath the bare maple and turned back to look at the house.

"Okay," he said, and then paused like he'd forgotten why he was there. "What do we have here..." He began looking in his folio for something, then kind of gave up and flipped it open to a blank sheet of graph paper.

"How old is the roof, Nick?"

"Oh, now, see, I don't know that. Bought the house three years ago and they didn't mention a new roof. I'd guess eight, ten, twelve years. I really don't know, Terry."

"That's fine," he said. "We'll take a look-see. Get the ladder out and go on up." Then Terry Locks just stood there a moment, looking at, or more likely past the roof. It was November, as I've said, and cold. Most of the leaves were already gone, and a mean wind was taking care of the stragglers. I thought maybe that was why Terry's eyes were watering. Then he fixed them on me, intensely, and he sort of bit his lower lip, like he needed steeling before going on.

"Good," I said. "Okay."

"Right," said Terry. "Right, I'll get the ladder." Then he brought a ladder from the back of his blue truck, a fold-up ladder that looked very light given how he was carrying it. He brought it up the driveway and began unscrewing the locking joints and straightening it out. He said nothing. Then, the ladder straight and locked, he leaned it up against the house, just above the front door, and put his right foot on the first rung.

"Here I go," he said.

"Okay," I said.

"Yep," he grunted, and vaulted up the ladder like a squirrel climbing a tree. Suddenly he was on the roof. He walked around a bit. I walked to the middle of the front lawn so that I could see him. He moved around slowly, saying, "Right, okay, yep." He took his tape measure off his belt, passed it from hand to hand, and clipped it back on.

"What's it look like up there?" I asked him, trying to spur him on. "How do those shingles look to you?"

"Total frigging devastation," he said, "like Hiroshima." What I thought, but did not say, was: What about Nagasaki? The bomb dropped on Nagasaki was bigger but everyone remembers Hiroshima. I guess it's more important to be first than to be bigger.

He walked around some more on spongy legs, like he was testing his own weightlessness. Once or twice he just put his head back and stared up at the sky with his knees flexed, and it looked for all the world like he was going to lose his balance and fall. I saw a man fall from a roof once. I was two hundred yards away when his ladder slipped out from under him. There was a clack and a flat thud. I watched the whole thing from a park across the street, and I remember being surprised by the rate at which he fell. I don't know what I expected; a wounded bird tumbling back to earth? But it was more like a Slushie thrown from an overpass.

I did nothing, just stared, took a few steps toward him, then felt like I could never get there in time to be of any help. His family filed out the front door and one by one gasped in horror. It wasn't a nice thing to see, and I didn't want to see it again, especially not on my own lawn.

But Terry Locks did not fall, thank goodness. He got his tape back out and he measured the roof first one way, and then the other, and then he inspected the flashing on the edge of the roof, and the chimney, and then he looked at all of the vents. He jotted things down on his pad. Over him the flat sky looked like a thing laid atop us, white and solid.

He lowered himself down the ladder with one hand, the other clamped onto his notepad, and in a moment he was folding up his ladder again. Then he sidled up the driveway and met me on the front step.

"I've got some numbers to run here," he said.

"Fine," I said.

"Could take a few minutes."

"Sure, okay."

Terry the roofing guy stood before me, seemingly uncertain. "Okay," he said, but he did not look okay. If ever a person did not look okay, it was Terry Locks as he stood on the front step of my home, swaying almost imperceptibly in the November wind. His face looked as though something behind it, something which should be girding it, had crumbled. His eyes were empty. I thought maybe he'd been drinking. It would explain the swaying.

"Do you want to come in," I asked him, "maybe have a seat while you run those numbers?"

"I think I would like to do that, Nick," he said. So we went inside where it was warm and bright.

Sometimes the weirdest things in the world don't seem weird at all while they're happening. It almost became a joke. He was sitting at the table so long, hunched over his notepad, that we sort of forgot he was there. Jordan came downstairs to show Terry some drawings he'd done.

"This is a dragon, but he can't fly. Are you the man who's going to fix our roof?"

"I might be that man," said Terry.

Every once in a while Ellie or I would ask Terry how the numbers were looking. The more we asked the more it became kind of a funny thing, and in time Terry was in on it. "Just a bit more figuring," he'd say, then laugh, or "You can't rush a man at his work, ha ha ha."

Soon Ellie was offering him afternoon tea. Before I knew it, Terry was sitting on the couch reading Jordan *The Gruffalo*, and doing a damn good job of it. His Gruffalo voice was impressive, it kept the boy in stitches.

The truth is nobody was really in a hurry to see Terry go.

After dinner he offered to help wash up. Once Jordan was in bed, Terry watched TV with us, laughing and making snide remarks just like we would. He was funny. He seemed a lot more at ease than he had been that afternoon. He had gone from tradesman to something more, which I suppose is what happens when you let a man put his feet up on your coffee table and watch your flatscreen for a few hours.

After the last medical drama of the evening, Ellie stood, stretched her little body out and up, and said, "I think I'm done for the night. Try to remember to get those numbers from Terry, won't you Nick?"

We all laughed, but then I thought, she's probably serious, so when she left the room I said to Terry, "I guess she's right about that, Terry. I'm sorry to push the matter along, but do you think I could get that quote now?"

He looked a bit taken aback, as though in having passed from tradesman to something more, he would never again be our tradesman. As though he wasn't even the same person who'd arrived earlier to give us a quote on a new roof. But then he said, "I've just got to write it all up. Let me go to the truck and I'll come back and run down the options with you."

"Fine," I said, and he put on his boots and coat and went out into the night. I heard his truck door open and then shut. When I heard it open again five minutes later I went down to the front door to meet him.

"Alright," he said, "here it is." He looked like an under-grad who'd fudged his way through a paper and was now handing it in. The sheet he gave me was stapled to a bro-chure for a particular brand of shingles as well as another business card. I parsed it. The number was a little higher than I'd expected, but it didn't shock me.

"Okay," I said, "Let me take this in."

"Because I feel like we're friends now," Terry said, "I should say that if you wanted to pay cash, straight cash, you know, I could do it for five thousand, all in."

"Five thousand."

"Right, uh huh. Quietly, of course."

"Of course."

"Either way, Nick, I know it's a lot of money. I don't take this lightly. I know it's hard to make these sorts of decisions," he said, like he was reading my mind, like it wasn't what anyone in this same situation would be feeling. It was a salesman's trick, and I didn't like him for pulling it out after all that had happened between us. "There's a lot of money involved, I get that. This sort of decision can weigh on a relationship," he said, "on a marriage. It can make you wonder, Who is this person I'm with? Can I trust her? Why does she resent me given all that I've done for her, all I've given up, okay?"

"Right," I said, but slowly, to show that I wasn't really following him down this particular trail.

"And maybe she's out a lot, or doesn't confide in you anymore."

"You're saying I should talk about it with Ellie," I said, trying to get things back on the rails.

"Exactly. I mean, if this is the sort of thing you two talk about. I don't know how this works for you, the dynamic. Like right now, for me, I'm sort of considering leaving my wife. Like, *today*. Or tonight, I guess, ha. So I wouldn't necessarily consult her about it, or anything now. But, you know. For you? And Ellie? I can't say."

There it is, I thought. It was like finding the pinhole in a tire that's slowly been losing air. "Why don't you come back in, Terry, and I'll find us some beers," I said. And the thought came to me, guiltily in the light of what Terry had revealed, that once this was over I was going to need another quote.

The first time Terry mentioned it, it sounded to me like a fundamentally bad idea, like carpeting in the bathroom. We were watching a loop of sports highlights for the second or third time. Goal-goal-goal-fight-goal. I was just coming back from the kitchen with a bowl of microwave popcorn for us to share. I had put some extra margarine on it and sprinkled it with Old Bay. I had two bottles of beer, one in each hip pocket of my jeans, and I had a roll of paper towels under my arm. Terry looked at me as I came out of the kitchen and he started to say something. I assumed it would be, "Need a hand?" But it wasn't. It was, "We should go away together."

"What?" I said as he cleared away our half-dozen empty bottles to make room for the new ones and the popcorn.

"Yeah, you know, somewhere without women, just for a while. I think I see what you need, Nick, and it's just what I need: space. Wood, water, trees!" he said, raising his arms.

"Right," I said. "Have another, Terry."

"Fish," he said. "I know you fish, don't you, Nick?"

"I do."

"Imagine the longest fishing trip you've ever been on, Nick. Think of living that way."

"Drink up, buddy," I told him, and I did the same.

Sometime past midnight I noticed that Terry had left me drinking alone. He'd gotten a stein from the kitchen and kept filling it with water from the filter jug in the fridge. Then he found the cookie dough ice cream and he had two or three bowls of that. All this time he kept peppering me with more and more enticing details of this scheme of his.

"That truck out there would last us years," he said. "It'd be ours."

"I've always wanted a truck," I said.

"I kind of figured."

And by that time of night when you stop looking at the clock because there's nothing on TV anyway, it had become *our* scheme, a thing we both shaped, brought more fully into being, a thing we both believed. We were watching one of those half-hour commercials for a "companionship phone line" when out of nowhere I blurted, "There's something about the company of men, isn't there?"

"Men get it," Terry said.

"I think priorities come into play," I said.

"There's a difference in expectations, Nick. A big difference."

"If men lived with men, they'd take turns taking out the garbage, for instance."

"You bet they would, Nick."

I chewed on that for a moment. I knew I was a bit drunk, but I thought Terry was alright. I felt as though I was thinking straight, anyway. I felt like I was capable of weighing fairly one thing against another.

"You own a gun, Terry?" I asked.

"My dad's. Beautiful gun. He taught me to shoot with it."

"Ever take down a moose?"

"Naw, you?"

"Not yet I haven't."

"Imagine it, though."

"I have," I said, "a thousand times."

"That's the kind of thing men do."

"C'mon," I said. "Get your boots on." I stood up, aimed the remote at the TV and shut it off.

"Really, Nick? I mean, you're for real here?"

"Yes, goddamn it," I said. "Get your boots on, Terry. Now." I put on my warmest coat and the boots I'd had for thirteen years. I was consciously not taking stock of everything else I was leaving behind. I was not hastily packing a bag. I had everything I needed, I thought, in the form of my wits, the clothes on my back, and the Swiss Army knife in my hip pocket.

"Won't she notice you're gone?" he asked.

"No," I said, then, "Yes. Shh. Just go, let's go."

And once we were out the front door, I had a feeling in my chest like the sound of a chainsaw starting up. There were magnesium flares going off in my blood. My pulse hammered in my throat and everything looked new. We ran down the driveway and jumped into the truck. I didn't look back at the house. I didn't look to see the soft glow of Jordan's night light in his window. I didn't look back to see if there was a face peeking through the curtains.

We were driving nowhere in particular, some dreamscape forest of the mind that we didn't bother to fix in real space. Anyway, there was a sense that a destination wouldn't really matter until dawn, until the morning light brought the world into sharper focus. I wasn't anxious for that time to come. Until then we'd just put some miles between us and whatever had come before. The next day was Saturday, and back at the house that meant a farm breakfast: bacon, pancakes, sausages, eggs, some sliced apples, juice, coffee. Ellie grew up on a farm in eastern Quebec and that had been their tradition, one she brought to the marriage. It was always a great pleasure to me, and I was sorry I wouldn't know it anymore. But maybe there'll be a diner somewhere ahead, I thought. It wouldn't be the same, but that was the point, wasn't it?

Terry's face was dimly lit by the dashboard glow, and he looked ten years younger than when I'd met him just the previous afternoon. He looked bright, fresh, hopeful, re-inflated. I wondered how I looked to him. Did I look like his brother? A friend? Did I look like a lover?

As we drove on that night, into the wide, inviting Canadian nowhere, toward whatever we were to become, the darkness behind us was the world dropping away from my feet, a great gulf opening there. It was unknown and frightening and I wished not to go back to it. I wanted only to be in the truck, with Terry. But I began to think of what I would say to Ellie if I ever spoke to her again. And I decided that what I would tell her was that sometimes the really big decisions, the ones we can't explain, are the best ones we ever make.

"Goddamn," I said to Terry. "Goddamn!"

FLORIDIANS

It's a common thing, I guess, to step off an airplane here and into a perfect, salty evening—the cries of seabirds, the sound of traffic humming by on the highway, the gentle rustling of the palms—and to wonder why a person would ever leave this place. To make a mental note to go back home and work for another thirty years, and then sell everything except a set of Callaways and a pair of deck shoes, and to move permanently down to Florida to wait out the end.

A common thing, maybe. But then a good many common things always eluded me.

The gleaming white taxicab tore along the four-lane, across the bay, then onto the causeway over to the Keys. The seat covers had lascivious-looking flamingos on them. The cars shone on the palm-lined causeway, and the Gulf wind kicked through the open window. Outside, I saw houses built close to the earth. An open-air laundromat and an adult video warehouse in a strip mall next to a giant home improvement store. A massive dog track, big as a football stadium. There was something chiming and bright on the radio, ours or someone else's.

I had arrived at this place looking for something. What I

sought was grace, only I didn't know it then. Instead, I said "fun," I said "relaxation." Anyone else might've just gone on a bender, but I didn't have the friends for that. I needed something to suggest that I had worth, whatever form that took, or if I had none, to learn how I might acquire it.

I'd always been wary of the whole state of Florida, thinking it little more than a big strip mall surrounded by water and sinking into swamp, full of bluehairs and the laughably conservative. But I'd wound up with a bit of time to kill, and I wanted to feel the sun's fullness in the dead of winter, so I let the wind and cheap airfare carry me south. I found a room at a place called The Sands at Indian Beach, and booked it for two months.

"No problem," said Mr. Beverley, the owner, who I'd reached by phone. "Just had new countertops installed."

And before I knew it, I was walking the beaches and dipping my ghostly white toes in the Gulf of Mexico, feeling a suspicion of easy leisure lift off my shoulders and disappear, replaced by a kind of goofy and easy hands-in-pockets gait, a loose and happy feeling of the sun on my face and arms.

I sought the banyan, the date palm, the sycamore, palmetto, mangrove. The roseate spoonbill, the pelican, the heron, ibis, egret, cormorant. Never the grotesque neon and cheap plastic, not the talcum and death smell of old people, not waiting in line while a woman insists on paying for her groceries with a personal cheque, not the traffic-choked roads. The birds and the trees: these are the things I wished to keep.

I took a cab to the state botanical gardens. I walked through them with my hands in my pockets and the dumbest smile on my face, smelling the floral notes so deep and rich they were almost vulgar. A couple stood by the tall grass and took pictures of an alligator with their zoom lens, debating whether or not the animal was real, lying there perfectly still fifty yards away. When it shook its tail and slid like oil into the water beneath the reeds the woman gave a small shriek.

That night I got ripping drunk in a place with fishing nets strung across the panelled ceiling and plastic fish hung in random constellations, because that's what you do in a strange town, isn't it? You find a bar and you sit among the blue-veined men who are talking college football and the governor's record on crime, and you drink a local beer in order to forge some connection to the place, drawing Xs and Os in the dewy runoff of your umpteenth bottle.

I made my wobbly way back to The Sands, to my room decorated with fish and sailboats and all manner of aquatically themed plastic things, and I watched a *Law & Order* rerun, then part of a dog show. A German wirehaired pointer with large, watery eyes stood like a painting at its handler's feet, perhaps seeking its own version of grace, but I fell asleep before they handed out the trophies.

At The Sands there's a long central corridor that runs through the building where you can gaze along the pink stucco walls and see the ocean, and in the evenings the sun would set right there. Sometimes I'd sit in a plastic kitchen chair outside my door at the end nearest the street and wait for the immodest pink and orange flare of sunset to appear there, framed by the stucco walls.

It was out of that corridor that I watched her walk one afternoon. She came from the direction of the ocean. I was reading by the pool, which was always empty. She took a lounge chair on the far side. It wasn't all that hot a day, a bit cloudy, but she wore small cut-offs and a bikini top. She looked at me over her magazine. It was a bored look, or maybe, if I were to summon some optimism, a look that said, You're the first not-boring thing to land here in a while.

I leaned back and looked up into the sky, watched an airliner slice into a cloudbank.

How strange to find yourself in a new place. How suddenly freeing to discover that things about you are different. To approach her instead of sitting on your hands. To make remarks funnier than you'd have thought you could muster. To manage small talk, even charmingly. To agree to her invitation to go to a blues club, even though you hate the blues. To do so not because of her enthusiasm, or her beauty, or not only her beauty, but also because you reason that what you hate is the blues clubs back home, or maybe that the person who hates blues clubs is the home-based you, a former being, a dead acquaintance.

Once there, your excitement is genuine. Your stomping foot, your hand on her knee under the table. The ease with which you address the waitress, the colourful drinks you order. What, you wonder, makes you the person you are? It's a feeling like falling, the pleasantness of shifting boundaries, of a night floating by without a moment of doubt or an instance of regret, dawn arriving to find you still awake, looking down at her hair on the pillow in the soft, soundless glow of sunrise. To be in this new place, and to make yourself anew away from those things people know and hold you to, all those personal contracts left far behind.

The next night we watched the sun go down from a place called Pier 60, up the key a ways. There were vendors selling cheap things, and a canteen counter with funnel cakes and soft drinks. An entertainer with a headset microphone walked among the crowd, juggling fire, telling jokes, and then pretended to steal my wallet. After, we walked out onto the pier as the darkness grew and the wind kicked up, listened to the surf hammer against the massive pilings buried deep in the Gulf sand.

I reserved a table for two at a nice seafood restaurant. I gave them the name Ted Cruikshank, which was the one I'd given her on a whim when we met by the pool. An alias felt, in that moment, like a potentially useful deception. The reasons were elusive even to me—I had no wife, no creditors, I wasn't hurting anyone. I just had the gut feeling that while living and moving about on this humid spit of land between sea and swamp I might engage in certain untidy acts with someone I might never intend to see again.

Did she ever see my credit cards? My driver's licence? I don't know. She never said anything. It's possible she did see them, but before speaking was reminded in some way of the matter of her age, a subject that, if I'm honest, we were both careful to avoid. I had my lie, and she had hers. The shared knowledge of both of these deceptions might have been all we ever really had in common.

It was all very good that night, everything in trim working order, propelled along by an unusually easy feeling. The lobster, the wine, the dim light, her laughter.

She asked, of course: What was I doing in Florida?

"Visiting," I said.

"Who?"

"You, as it turns out." At this she blushed.

"Well, how long are you staying?"

I took a sip of wine. "I don't know. Maybe a couple of months."

And how exactly, she asked, did a person my age find

himself with all this time and money, seemingly, to burn? On this count I gave her the truth, more or less: the IT company where I'd been a programmer had been swallowed by a big American competitor, and I and most of my fellow programmers had been deemed extraneous. As I had developed a key piece of the software which had made the little fish so attractive to the big fish, and the former owner being understandably grateful, I was handed a compensatory cheque for a sum falling somewhere beyond generous but perhaps just short of princely. I was wished good luck, and sent away.

"Look," I said to her, "I'm under thirty, no kids, single. I was standing on a street corner in Toronto in the middle of February, which—I don't know if you've ever been anywhere like that, but—the blowing snow, the wind was howling. So I said, 'Screw this,' went home, fired up my laptop, bought a one-way ticket, and here I am."

She smiled, ran her birdlike fingers through her sandy-blonde hair. "Wow, you're a lucky guy."

"I can't deny that," I said, and I could feel us sliding toward something irretrievable.

Deep in the night, as we slept in my room, there was a flash, a shower of sparks outside the condo's window, and by the time we were conscious there was a ruckus out there. Three fire trucks arrived as we crept in the dark and opened the blinds, straining our necks for a better view. Finally I went outside in my bare feet while Stephanie stood in the doorway of my room. She folded her shapely arms and hunched her small shoulders against the chill.

"It's just a little fire," she whispered. "Come back inside."

But I didn't. With the cool pavement underfoot I went out into the parking lot, where I watched men in firefighting gear direct traffic, rerouting cars as they kept clear of the live wires now lying across the street. The transformer atop the pole nearest our building had exploded, the wires severed, flopping. The top of the pole still burned. There was a short man standing near me. "It was the damnedest thing," he said, offering his story to me with a confessional urgency. "I was watching CNN and I saw it happen right out that window. Just a big flash, then the bang. I called them," and he pointed to the fire trucks. "'Stay outside until they arrive,' they tell me on the phone. Then they come and they're yelling at me, 'Get inside! Live wires!'"

I stood with the man, who I guessed from his Seminoles T-shirt, his drawl, and his deep tan, was either native to the state or a longtime visitor, which may amount to the same thing. While the firefighters stood around waiting for the utility people to arrive, he and I stood side by side watching the pole smoulder, a spent matchstick against an inky sky, a pair of men too tired to sleep, and the fire trucks with their lights flashing in the swollen Floridian night.

It might have been the next day, or the day after that, that Gary Holsapple, the pool and handyman at The Sands, and Stephanie's father, first spoke to me. I'd seen Gary before. Sometimes he'd be crouched before a flower bed or an electrical panel, a bandana spilling from the back pocket of his dirty Lee jeans, a Tampa Bay Buccaneers cap up on his big, damp head. I'd hear him tinkering, or explaining a problem to himself, or breathing heavily just outside the window of my kitchenette. I'd say hello in passing, or mention the weather, or heap praise on the shape of the place. He'd nod without saying a word.

Early on in this whole mess I tried to will myself into believing Stephanie might be as old as twenty-one, but in the end that proved useless. Let's be perfectly honest about this: I knew.

I was standing on the beach, between the Gulf and The Sands, watching sandpipers tease the surf, thinking about Stephanie, maybe even wondering idly about her age, when a big, leathery hand clamped over my shoulder.

"Let's you and me talk," he said.

He walked ahead of me, lumbering, and led me toward the building, down the central corridor, and past the pool, to what I quickly figured was his condo. He knows, I thought. He knows and he's going to kill me. There was maybe something in his waistband. A shape. It looked solid, like the butt of a gun.

He unlocked his door and I mutely followed him inside. I stood in the doorway of the home of a large American man, a labourer, whose daughter I had touched and kissed and driven to restaurants and bought wine. Whose clothes I had removed. I stood in his home and wondered what kind of gun he had tucked into the back of his Lee jeans.

He motioned toward a flowery sofa. "Have a seat." To my own surprise, I did. And while I did I tried to remember what I'd read about the screwy laws in Florida. By entering his home, had I just given him permission to kill me? Was I an intruder? Was he within his rights to shoot me and claim he'd only been standing his ground?

"Get you anything?" he asked.

"No," I said.

"Sorry, we haven't actually been introduced." He offered me his hand. "Gary Holsapple."

"Ted," I said, and cut myself short of offering the fraudulent surname.

"Yeah. Ted. Get you anything?"

"Thanks, no."

"Coke? Sprite?"

"I'm fine," I said through the lump in my throat. He was proving to be an awfully friendly instrument of death.

He went into the kitchen area, just to the back of the condo, swung open the fridge and got himself a Diet Coke. He walked back toward me, cracked the can open, and sat on the recliner opposite the couch. He was quiet a moment. The place smelled like carpet cleaner.

"Stephanie's seventeen, you know," he said.

"Stephanie?"

"Stephanie. My daughter, your new friend. She's seventeen."

"Really? I didn't—"

"Reason I'm saying this is, you're not. Are you?" He sipped his Coke.

"Me? No. Not seventeen."

"Right. I know. Hold on," he said, and he stood, put his drink on a glass-topped wicker side table, and left the room. I flinched visibly as he walked by. My vision tunnelled in then, and my body broke out in a sweat. I became dizzy and I believed that the room itself had changed colour and tilted about forty-five degrees.

When, in a moment, he returned not with a knife or a club or a roll of plastic sheeting, but with a book in his hands, I was relieved and confused. It was a photo album, its cover pink and flocked, like the fur of a stuffed bear. The cover read OUR LITTLE PRINCESS. He sat next to me on the couch and opened the album.

"There she is," he said, pointing to a photo of a tiny girl in white-blonde pigtails. "God. Adorable." If he was going to shoot me I wished he would just up and do it. But instead he kept turning the album's stiff, heavy pages, showing me more and more photos of Stephanie as a chubby toddler, Stephanie at Disney World, Stephanie as a gangly pre-teen. What cut me the most was just how well I remembered the years suggested by the decor in the pictures, the slogans and graphics on her T-shirts, the style of her running shoes.

"My little girl," Gary Holsapple said.

"Mr. Holsapple, I—"

"Gary."

"Gary. Look, I think I understand what you're trying to say," I said, then tried to chuckle. "And yes, okay, consider it done. I'm sorry about the whole thing. If you'd like me to find somewhere else to stay, I can do that, too. I was thinking about heading home any—"

"Just be careful with my little girl's heart, is what I'm saying."

"What?" I said, but he was distracted. He'd come to a photo at the end, which showed Stephanie perhaps only months younger than she was when I'd met her. She was sitting on the hood of her powder blue VW Rabbit, in short shorts and a tank top, flashing a peace sign.

"God, she's beautiful, isn't she?" he said. "She looks so much like her mother, rest her soul. Mrs. Holsapple was about that age when I met her, too. They're hard to resist, aren't they?"

"Wow."

"Ted, listen. I know she comes off wise and sharp, all that. Wild, a bit tough. A big girl. But you remember being that age, don't you? She's just a kid. Be careful with her. Do you understand me?"

"Okay, yeah."

"A father needs to know his baby is going to be taken care of."

"Of course."

"Good," he said. "Good!" And he stood, and stepped toward me. "I'm glad we had this talk, Ted." He opened his big arms to welcome me into a kind of collegial embrace. Two men, fools each, promising the safeguarding of a woman. A girl. He took me into his immense chest and I in turn wrapped my arms around his waist, and I moved my hands there, looking for the hard thing, the lump, the butt of a Colt, or a Sig Sauer, or a Glock. But I found nothing. Only fabric, and the leather of Gary's belt.

That night Stephanie came to my room and when I opened the door she flounced in and sat across the loveseat in a manner not unprovocative.

"So you talked to Daddy," she said.

"I did. Nice man. Where's he from, originally?"

"Akron."

"Do people from Ohio shoot people from Canada?"

"What are you even talking about, oh my god."

"Historically, I mean."

"Come on," she said.

"Where are we going?"

"You'll see," she said. I changed and we fell into her Rabbit and headed off. We hadn't gone ten blocks when she spotted a yard sale, wheeled around, and pulled up curbside.

"I love old junk," she said.

It was a street sale, a dozen or more houses spilling their musty contents onto folding card tables, women and men in lawn chairs taking bills for paperbacks, old golf shoes, furniture, board games. I stood shoulder-to-shoulder with bargain-hunters, sun-worshippers, registered Republicans, content Floridians. Their complaints, their laughter, their haggling all amounted to the same thing: "How will I forestall death?" And the fiery sunsets, the massive weather patterns like airborne continents looming over the Gulf, the storms being born in the Caribbean and churning their way north all contend: "You can't."

This is what Stephanie, for all her youthful beauty, will become. And, were I to, say, stick around here and marry this girl, this is what I, too, would become. It wouldn't be better than life at home, despite the sun, despite the bikinis. It would take the same form of talk radio morning commutes, constant residual frustration like an almost undetectable white noise, doubt, moments of sudden exhaustion in wide-aisled grocery stores when my whereabouts and purpose temporarily escape me.

Say I made Stephanie my bride, Mrs. Ted Cruikshank—for the lie would have to be upheld, wouldn't it? Thirty years from now, our intimacy long since having slipped away, a young girl might walk by on the beach wearing something she'd hidden from her parents, and something would move in me, a stirring in the old machinery. Shame and hot intimations of death, of wasted years, of animosity and self-hatred, and simple, animal impulse. God, how awful I would be, and how I'd hate Stephanie for allowing—or causing—me to become this leathery, sausage-limbed cartoon. Her tiny feet toughened and wrinkled. My right-leaning voting habits. And our children? Shipped off to FSU on track scholarships or academic bursaries. Our weekend air-conditioned Cadillac trips to school functions, to stadiums, wearing matching caps and sweatshirts, screaming "Go Seminoles" until we were hoarse. Weddings in Tampa-St. Pete. Family steak dinners in chain restaurants off I-75. Burial in a swamp.

Stephanie's street sale purchase was a mustard yellow

suede handbag that looked depressingly like something my own mother used to carry. We got back into the Rabbit and pulled away from the curb.

"Was that where you wanted to take me?" I asked.

"God no," she said. "I just saw that. We're going for the best grouper sandwiches in the world."

Life is not composed of what we do, but of what we miss. I had then my first and, as it would happen, only glimpse of an Old Florida, the Spanish-moss draped enclave of the deep South, as we drove slowly down a shaded side street lined with once-great homes, arcaded, stuccoed—now crumbling and sagging, gardens reclaimed by the tangle and muck. A very old woman sat motionless in a chair on a down-sloping verandah in a queer greenish light, a small dog in her lap.

I had no way of knowing that I would not see that version of the world again, but something tugged gently downward on my heart then. I must have recognized that my contact with that hidden place could only ever prove fleeting, casual, and it stung me in the manner of personal loss. Most often and most painfully such things come to you in retrospect, but I felt it in that very moment, driving slowly by in Stephanie's rustbucket VW, on our way to get what she promised me would be a sandwich I would not ever forget.

That night, in Ybor City, we danced. In buildings that were once cigar factories, now made over into nightclubs, we drank. In the very early morning we walked cobblestone streets that had once been Tampa's Latin district, but were now the places where tourists searched in vain for something authentic. We searched for pizza, for margaritas, for cigarettes, for a place to lie down.

We tossed pennies into a fountain, made feeble wishes. And what did I wish for? What does anyone wish for, finally, after the wasted pleas for expensive things? A long and happy life. And the simple solution to the mess I'd found myself in: the soothing, seamless words necessary to extricate myself from this girl, her father, this condo, this state.

In the end I simply told her we were done. I left her a message. Sorry, I said. It had been a mistake. I left one for Beverley, too, asking him to call and tell me what I owed him. I placed the key on the counter of the kitchenette, got in a taxi, and was driven to the airport. And as the cab sped along, I said to myself it was okay, because I was never going to return to Florida again.

I ate a cellophane-wrapped sandwich while I watched CNN on a giant screen in the terminal, beneath an enormous pelican suspended by cables from the ceiling above.

Seventeen.

We boarded, and the plane taxied away from the terminal for what seemed a great while, then squared its shoulders to the designated runway. It powered up and began its hard acceleration. The sound filled my head, rattled my teeth and sinuses. I felt my stomach in my feet, glanced out the window at the blur, and then the receding ground, the swamp and sand and highways, green and brown. There was a shudder then, a small one, minor but unmistakable, followed by a larger one. It was a sideways shimmy, a break in the continuity of our forward velocity. It felt distinctly wrong, as though in the middle of staring down gravity we had blinked. And then who were we? We were seventy-eight souls—seventy-eight names recorded on the passenger manifest, seventy-eight beautiful accidents of timing, tissue, love—falling back to Florida as quickly as we had left it.

BELOW THE LIGHTED SKY

We were on our way to a concert in Wakefield, Quebec, which is a village up in the Gatineaus, not far from Ottawa. There was a little pub and inn called the Blue Moose there, a place where semi-prominent musicians gave concerts to a small room full of people. The economics of the thing seemed dubious, but the musicians kept coming.

It is true that obscure musicians played there, too, and I suppose the band that we were going to see qualified as that. Spiderbite were from Louisville, Kentucky, and they played a kind of music which sounded as though your favourite punk rock cassette had been left in the sun, and then dropped into the bathtub.

It was the late autumn of 1992, and we were barely in our twenties. Four of us packed into a 1980 Volvo wagon on a high, cool day, the sky a severe blue, a wind from the north bringing with it the earliest hints of winter. Gavin Harkness was driving. It was his car, one he'd bought for $500 when he was touring under the name Rat Lee, an act which involved him plugging his guitar into a complicated arrangement of pedals for delay and distortion which he would then activate by crawling all over the floor on his hands and knees. He played shows for a year, from Hamilton to Montreal, Columbus, Ohio to Burlington, Vermont, and recorded a cassette he sold at venues, before retiring the name. But he still had the car.

In the backseat was Donald Hewitt, an aspiring writer who typed up and photocopied record reviews and emotional reactions to shows he'd attended, folded and stapled them into zines he'd mail out all over the place. He was earnest and skinless. I suppose we all were. Tara Shaw sat next to him, a sardonic, serious, and dark young woman with a tattooed chain of paper dolls encircling her right bicep.

At the time I was living in a strange, rundown house with seven other young men above a jam space in the basement. I worked in a bakery, a job which I hated and which paid poorly, but I lacked ideas as to what else I might do. Everyone I knew was underfed and frail. We had prescriptions— pill bottles, inhalers, EpiPens for our varying ailments. Donald had to stay away from bees, nuts, and milk. Tara's veganism left her anemic.

But what really bound us was that we all listened to the same bands. My older brother Philip called it "music for depressives," a term I rejected but, if pushed, would've admitted was apt. The music and the scene surrounding it appealed to introverted kids who lacked drive, athletic ability, and social skills.

In some cases it is true that kids were the way they were because of bad homes, bad diagnoses, bad teachers. There was an undercurrent of nihilism against which I halfheartedly struggled. All the boys I knew had given up skateboarding in order to sit in dark rooms and listen to bands like Spiderbite. We became serious and dour. We did not smoke or drink.

It was oppressive, but there was something about it which felt safe to me, and it didn't ask me to do things that made me uncomfortable. So I bought the records and went to the shows. Shows in basements, shows in Legion halls, in churches, in small, dark, damp clubs where these bands had to split time with metal acts and classic rock revivalists. The scene accepted my introversion and my timidity. It encouraged them. I found a community of people who, like me, basically lacked direction. The scene became our direction.

The geese were leaving, lifting up from the fields and moving in their great formations toward the south. It was late in the day and the cold sunlight slanted away from us as we drove out of Ottawa, across the bridge and into Quebec. We drove north and the city dropped away and we were among the deep reds and oranges of the changing leaves in the hills. The Volvo rattled and clapped. Gavin removed one cassette from the dashboard and shoved in another. Drums began thudding and a heavy guitar chainsawed away.

"Is this Crimpshrine?" Donald asked from the back seat.

"Yeah," said Gavin. "Some of their early songs."

"I don't know," Donald said after a moment, "I feel like maybe some of this stuff is hyped up because of who was involved, not because of how good it was."

"Is that how you feel, Donald?"

Donald shifted about, sat up straighter in his seat. "Yeah."

Gavin twisted his fists over the steering wheel. "Okay."

"It's got all this Bay Area feel to it, but, like, it's not really political or anything."

"Tell me, Donald," Gavin said, "Tell me what to think

of them."

"Relax, Gavin," said Tara, "he's just expressing his opinion."

"He's always just expressing his opinion," said Gavin, and kept driving.

The highway was easy enough; take the autoroute from Hull right up into the Gatineaus. Once we turned off, though, things became complicated. We each sighted landmarks we were certain pointed the way, but those landmarks were all different, and we couldn't agree on which way they led.

"No," Gavin said, "there's a parking lot for the ski trails, and then you go up that way." He pointed to a road that wound up a hillside.

"We need to be on the other side of the highway," Tara said. "I'm sure of it."

Gavin, I had the sense, didn't think she was right, but as he'd been trying unsuccessfully to kiss Tara for three or four years, he seemed to think it best to listen to her. We turned around and drove across the overpass, to the other side of the highway.

"Now go left, I think?" Tara said.

The sunlight was leaving, only long shadows remained, and the odd shard of cold, yellow light. There were a few farmhouses there, little cottages among the trees. The road grew smaller, and then it was a gravel road.

"Probably not the right way, I'm guessing," said Donald.

"That's what you think, is it, Donald?" said Gavin.

"Relax, Gavin," said Tara.

Gavin took a right, another gravel road, shooting between walls of trees.

"Where are you going?" I asked.

"I'll take this until we hit the river, then follow it up," he said. "Sound good to everybody?"

"Sure," said Donald.

"Whatever," said Tara.

"Good," said Gavin, "because that's what I'm doing."

The sun had slipped completely below the hills by then. Everything was swimming in a suffocating blue dimness. The Volvo's headlights didn't seem to be doing any good. Behind us the hills were all in shadow, and the forests between fields had become black.

Gavin had slowed the car because the road was terribly rutted and the light was so bad. We dipped and rose, then veered around a steep bend, between two open fields. Gavin seemed bored, or aggravated, and when he cleared the bend he mashed the Volvo's accelerator.

"Whoa," said Donald. Tara grabbed the door handle next to her, braced her other hand on the seat. The Volvo fishtailed and shimmied across the loose gravel, jounced and shuddered. We hopped over a little bump and I hit my head on the passenger side window.

Tara said, "Ow! Gavin, slow it down!"

I looked over my shoulder at Donald and Tara when I felt a sudden hiccup, and then heard a terrific whistling noise. The tail of the car snaked its way along behind us, and the road began to feel spongy.

"Shit," said Gavin quietly. The car slowed and he eased it to a stop on a muddy strip next to the road, right up against a split-rail fence. We all sat in silence for a moment, then two, then three. "We have a flat," he said, his hands still clamped on the steering wheel. He was the oldest among us, but he looked young then. He wore a thrift store toggle coat that smelled like mothballs, black corduroy pants and, like all of us, all-black high-top Converse. But as he looked out over the steering wheel, at the road where it disappeared into the blue darkness, he looked like a kid. He undid his seatbelt, opened his door and stood in the road. He walked around the car and inspected the rear tire on the passenger side. We filed out of the car and stood near him, just looking at it.

"Anybody know how to change a tire?" Gavin said.

"Don't you?" Donald said. "It's your car."

"I've never done it," Gavin said.

"But you know how," said Tara.

"Yeah. Well, like, you unscrew one and put on the other."

"Unscrew?" I said.

Gavin twisted one hand over his other, which he held in a fist. "Unbolt."

"Where's the other?" said Donald.

"The trunk?" I said, having some vague notion that that was where one found the spare tire in a car.

"There's no tire in the trunk," Gavin said. "I'd have seen it."

The wind was cold and the ground seemed hard. There were no houses on that stretch of road and the fields had fallen into darkness. We were alone out there, without knowing just where there was. Without saying why, Gavin climbed over the split-rail fence and began walking into the field. We just watched him for a long while.

Finally Tara said, "Where is he going?"

"Nowhere," I said. I felt as though he was just moving, because moving was all he could do. It seemed likely to me that he was feeling as I did: that we'd had everything done for us, our whole lives. And now, out in the world, we'd been left to tally up a list of all those things of which we were incapable, one by one, as they came to us. Simple repairs. Filing taxes. The care and maintenance of automobiles. So we retreated. We'd reached the point where struggle and effort were necessary to propel ourselves forward into life, and as we knew very little about those things, or how to wield them to our advantage, we folded inward.

"Maybe he thinks tires grow out there," Donald said.

"This is so messed up," I said.

After a long time Gavin came walking back to us and stood on the other side of the fence, leaning his elbows on it. "I think we should walk that way," he said, jerking his head over his shoulder, indicating back across the field.

"Why would we do that?" asked Tara.

"Because what else do we do?" asked Gavin. He knew it was a bad idea, and he knew we all knew. Action for action's sake. But because he was the oldest and it was his car, we all listened. We began walking.

We had made two bad decisions—turning off the good roads and not stopping to ask directions—and then several smaller bad decisions followed until we found ourselves unable to get back to the junction of good sense and poor judgment. We were stranded out there, but nobody said it quite yet. We just walked across the muddy cool field and into a row of tall poplars, and then into another field. We walked and walked, and then Donald stopped and said, "We should stop. We should go back to the car and wait out the night."

"No. We should sleep in the fields," Gavin said.

"That's a terrible idea," said Tara, but he had turned and was marching quickly back toward the car. "Gavin," she cried, "there must be a house around here somewhere," echoing what I'm sure Donald and I were thinking. But Gavin kept on. He walked fast through the trees and across the first field, hopped the fence, then opened the Volvo's trunk. He pulled out an old weathered grey blanket, then a blue nylon tarp.

"You can have softness, or you can have waterproof. Pick."

"What is that?" asked Tara.

"Your bed," Gavin said, throwing her the tarp.

"Oh, perfect. Come on, Lyle," she said to me, climbing over the fence. "Let's go to bed."

Tara had chosen a spot among the poplars, overlooking the wet field. It was a little hump of dried grasses, shielded from the wind by a small berm. She arranged the tarp there, laying it flat, then sitting on it and pulling the lower half over herself.

"Why here?" I asked

"Because it's far away from Gavin." She patted the space next to her. I sat down, pulled my knees to my chest, and rocked a bit. She lay down.

"Relax," she said, so I tentatively unfolded myself and spread out on my side with my back to Tara.

"I feel bad about leaving Donald back there with Gavin," I said.

"You feel bad about everything, Lyle," she said, and she was not wrong.

"Gavin might kill him," I said.

"Donald's a big boy. Not your problem."

"What's Gavin's deal?" I asked, since Tara had known him longer than I had.

"Who knows. Absent father? Untapped aggression? Bad combination of meds? He was really into wrestling a few years ago. He's got stuff bottled up."

"I guess." I could feel the cold that was coming, which would settle into our bones as the night wore on. The poplars brushed against one another and hissed over our heads. There were stars visible up there, and if I looked out over the field, the speckled wash of the Milky Way.

"If you come closer we might stay a bit warmer."

"I just didn't know," I said, "like, if you wanted that."

"I don't want freeze to death," she said. "And, you know, some closeness might be nice. It would be hard to feel worse right now."

I slid myself back toward her, my knobby spine only just pressing into her side. "There," she said. "Romantic."

"Very," I said, and forced a laugh. I lay there with my muscles tensed in a way that was very uncomfortable, but I did not know that I could stop it. I was not yet too cold. The tarp was keeping us dry and warm, and I could feel the heat coming off of Tara, but I was terrifically afraid of getting too close to her, or of making her aware of my body. I was attracted to Tara, but not all that specifically. She was pretty and funny, but more importantly for me at that point in my life, she listened to The Nation of Ulysses and Spiderbite and enjoyed going to shows. That alone made her desirable. And being attracted to her made all my own flaws that much more important to conceal. How thin my arms were, how sharp my elbows, how bony my shoulders. My bad skin and my gamy body. I wrapped my arms around my knees and tried to hide them all from her.

Then Tara turned on her side, facing my back, and moved into me. She slid her arm around my ribcage and squeezed. I tensed up even more.

"Just relax, Lyle," she said, but I couldn't, and I have spent the years since trying to shake that suspicion of happiness, that fear of letting go.

After a time I realized Tara's breathing had levelled out and her grip on my body had slackened. I closed my eyes and tried to sleep, too, but the wind and the small movements of things, rustling and bird sounds, and the absurdity of our predicament—made worse by just how avoid-able it had been—kept me from it. So I turned my head and strained my eyes to look upward without disturbing her, and I looked at the stars.

Donald came crashing over. I could hear him moving across the field, stumbling and wheezing. He wasn't panicked, but he was agitated.

"Donald?" I said, which startled Tara awake.

"Jesus," she said.

"Fucking Gavin," he whispered, as though Gavin were right behind him, but I looked and could see no one coming across that first field, and I couldn't hear anything.

"What did he do?" I asked, looking Donald over for signs of molestation.

"He just won't stop talking about weird shit," Donald said, "like, famous murders and stuff."

"Creep," Tara said.

"Total creep," Donald said. "I'm just trying to sleep. Or at least not hear about Ted Bundy and The Zodiac while I lie in a Volvo in the middle of nowhere. Do you guys have any room?" He was already moving onto my corner of the tarp.

"I don't know," I said, "Maybe?"

Once Donald had settled in next to me there seemed no sense in even thinking about sleep. The three of us sat upright with the tarp pulled up to our chins, and we talked. We tried to imagine the show we were missing. We talked about camping, which seemed related to our current experience. We talked about our parents and when we had last wanted to go camping with them.

Then we heard the Volvo's door open on its creaky hinge, and shut with a clap.

"Oh great," Tara said, "he's coming to see us." I tried to imagine just how far away the car was, and how long the walk would take. In the dark everything seemed farther off.

After a while Gavin was nearly upon us. He was whistling something as he moved across the field and into the tree break. Then he stood over us.

"What are you guys doing out here?" he asked.

"Just hanging out," Donald said.

"Seems like a hell of a party," Gavin said. "My invitation must have been lost in the mail."

"Pull up some tarp," Tara said unconvincingly, but Gavin was still standing and had moved in front of us, looking out at the darkened field.

"Do you guys hear that?" he asked.

"What?" Donald said, and he started to his feet.

"Sshh. That. Honking."

"Geese?" I said.

"A ton of geese," said Gavin.

We all stood then, folding back the tarp and brushing imaginary things from our clothing. We gazed over the starlit field and let the shapes take their form as we all realized that we were looking at a flooded field full of thousands of geese resting on the shallow water. They had been so quiet. I'd had no idea they were there in such numbers. We stood looking at them, careful not to move or disturb them. They were barely visible, but came into sharper view the longer you looked. They sat on the water, which looked like lighter patches of darkness, reflecting the sky back up, and some of them turned in slow circles, while others were completely motionless. There came a honk or two, lazy little noises you could not attribute to any one animal, out there in the flat, dark field.

"Look at the pretty geese," Gavin finally said. "All those pretty, pretty geese." His voice trailed off and he lingered on the final consonant in a way that sounded sinister. "Our dads would be shooting them. It would be like target practice." He raised his right hand to his shoulder and held his left out in front of him, elbow crooked, as though holding a rifle. "Boom," he whispered.

"Too bad we've got nothing to shoot them with," said Donald.

"Oh, but we don't shoot," said Gavin, his voice loud. "Right? What are we, Americans? If we had a gun in the trunk, would you shoot all the birds?"

"No. What for?" said Donald.

"Just to kill them. Would you, Donald? Come on, would you?" Something was rising in Gavin. He had turned and was facing Donald, his back to the field of geese. "How about a fucking machine gun? Huh? Take them all out? Tat-tat-tat-tat-tat!" He was shouting now, and the geese were stirring.

"No."

"A knife, then," he said. "A fucking knife! You could sneak up and cut their throats." He drew a knife from his pocket that none of us knew he had. It was long and impressive when he unfolded it, with a blade that curved slightly, and a slender tip. It looked like a relic, something from the bottom of a trunk, or a museum display case.

"Oh my god," said Donald, and even in the darkness I could see that his already pale face had gone the colour of paper.

Tara said, "What the hell, Gavin?"

Gavin said nothing. He held the knife straight up in the air in front of his face, between him and Donald, and he stared at the tip of it. We all stared at the knife.

"Sometimes you need a knife," he said, "that's the truth,

even if you don't like it." He waved it around. "But some-times you have to cut something!"

"Put it away, Gavin," Tara said. "We get it, you're scary. Now put it away."

He held it at the very bottom of the grip, between his thumb and index finger. He let it waggle there, and then dropped it. It stuck in the ground at our feet, straight up-right. "Fine. You won't forget I have it, though." He picked up the knife and wiped the blade on his pants.

He was right about that. I felt our vulnerability to blades, to the cold, to our own ignorance, standing out there in a dark field in west Quebec. Gavin had folded the knife and put it in his pocket, but we couldn't put it away. As we ac-cumulated knowledge of the world's threats, we could not go back and pretend to be the children we'd recently been.

I've had my own children since then, and I have worried about them the way I know my parents helplessly worried about me. I looked at our newborn twin boys and I said to my wife, "They're beautiful, aren't they? Look at what we did. They're beautiful." And she looked at me and said, "Now what do we do?"

I had no answer then, but what I would say now is that if a person can look at his children when they are grown and say, "They're a better version of me," that would be okay. A person could be happy with that. If he can say, "I kept them safe."

But we are out in the world, and we cannot be sure of the intentions of others. There are so many things for which we cannot account. It all requires such luck that I am amazed we make it through at all, any of us.

"Gavin," Tara said, "I think we'd all feel better if you didn't have that knife."

"Worried I'll go all Dahmer on you?"

"Kind of, yeah," she said, and he laughed. Tara was the only one of us who could talk to him like that, and he knew we knew that.

"Do you want to keep it?" he asked.

"Yes, please," Tara said. He took it from his pocket and handed it to her, and she held it behind her back. We stood facing the field of geese, me a step behind her, and I could see in the faint light the shape of the knife in her fist. As she held it, the knife seemed to lose its heat and menace, to become an ordinary thing, uncharged. A piece of metal with which you might cut meat, or slice a length of rope. A utilitarian object. It was, in fact, Gavin's unpredictability which had made the moment so tense, and that was still present. He still held that.

We made our way back to the car, which Gavin ran for a while with the heat up all the way, and we wrapped up in the tarp and the blanket, not speaking. We dozed fitfully until the light came and the rising sun began setting the tops of the hills ablaze.

Gavin and I were standing behind the car in the dim early morning when a man in a pickup truck came by. He stopped and helped us find the spare under the floor of the trunk, and put it on. He shook his head and laughed at us, which was fair. We were silly young people, hungry and tired. Once the spare was on he wished us luck getting back to the city.

We drove in the new light, the sun just reaching over the hills as we retraced our steps and found the autoroute. The road seemed to roll out ahead of us and drop away. None of us spoke. Soon, all of the valley opened before us. There below the fresh and airy sky lay Ottawa, scene of our failures and conflicts, our home and the place where we hoped to identify success, if not to experience it. It appeared static and distant. It looked untouchable, even unfathomable in its complexity. Roads and buildings and the grinding of machinery.

We drove through Hull and then across the Alexandra Bridge, with Parliament Hill visible off to our right. Gavin took us east toward the Byward Market to drop Donald off first at his apartment in Vanier, then he'd take me downtown, and finally deliver Tara to her apartment in Lowertown. It was a route that made sense only when you considered Gavin's feelings for her.

No one had spoken. It was oppressively quiet in the Volvo. The tape deck was on but the volume was very low. I don't even know what was playing. Minor Threat? Cap'n Jazz? We caught weekend traffic in the Market and crawled slowly through it. It was busy, people walking, people on bicycles. Perhaps one of the last bright days before the snow came. People moved easily. The air was cool, but fresh.

We stopped at a light, near the corner of the old market building, and there was a crowd of people there. I rolled down the passenger-side window and heard music. I stabbed the eject button on the Volvo's tape deck.

There was a band surrounded by people standing in a semicircle. The band was playing a U2 song, "Where the Streets Have No Name." I could see their small amplifiers through a break in the crowd. The light stayed red and I watched and listened.

"Kill me now," said Gavin. "Is that U2?"

"It's a cover band," said Donald. "Mad Market, or something. They're always playing down here. People love that crap."

The guitarist was sawing away and his guitar had a ringing, sustained quality to it. He strummed and strummed as the music rose and the crowd bent their knees. The stoplight stayed red for what seemed like forever. I leaned out the window of the Volvo, my elbows bent, chin resting on my wrists, and I watched. I wanted to see what was happening. I wanted to watch those four young men play music and entertain a crowd of people on a brisk, sunny Saturday morning. The band all had long hair in ponytails, and baggy hooded sweaters and jeans. The guitarist's sweater was tie-dyed. The singer wore a bandana and sunglasses and he held his microphone with both hands as he stepped forward. He seemed both earnest and showy.

"I want to run..." he sang.

I can see myself there as though this was all a movie that I am watching today. I can see my sallow skin and my sunken eyes, my short, severe hair. I can see the disapproving looks on the faces of Gavin and Donald. I can see myself as I was then, inward-looking, lost, watching a band play a U2 song on a street corner, and I can see the people gathered around them looking attentive, not walking by, but stopping and waiting for something to be expressed to them. And I am looking out that car window in that interval between red and green. Twenty-one years old. I want to talk to myself as I was then. I want to say, Look at those people. How do they differ from you? Can you imagine what it is to be them? Look at them smiling and slapping their thighs. I want to ask my younger self: Do they look happy? Do they look like they know what happiness is?

LIGHTER THINGS

This is where we're at: the wind has been up for twenty-three days now. Not gusty, but up, steadily. It just swung around one afternoon and began pouring out of the east. It's normal, of course, for the wind to blow hard through the spring and the early summer, but not like this.

Our house, a stout, plain farmhouse, sits on the soft hills that roll southward to Rice Lake, which appears to us as a blue smudge through the trees that ring it. But those trees are bent nearly horizontal now, and the house feels as though it has developed a lean. The wind hammers against the walls and it has torn off the shutters, the antenna, bits of the trim. I consider it a miracle that nothing has yet come through the glass.

I am a daughter of this place and this soil which is blowing away. My husband comes from a family that farmed tobacco near Leamington, but he came here to be with me. For twenty-six years we have put our beans in the ground but this year the wind took them all. All the seed. The wind scoured the fields bare and then began digging away at what was beneath our hill. We have learned that our hill contains the past, and all we had forgotten is buried there.

The bones of a cat. Rusted things. Boxes and suitcases and old wooden crates. The lighter things—unsent postcards, legal documents, the adult magazines I discovered beneath mattresses, the love letters, the motel receipts—flap violently and are gone almost before they can be identified.

Our three sons have grown and left us, but we see them in our hill, too, in what has been exposed. Stolen video game cartridges. Keys to the Oldsmobile that Joshua wrecked. Parts from the Ski-Doo David lost beneath the lake's ice. Henry's hockey gear. Pocket knives and BB guns.

At night we lie still and wonder what we will find peeking above the dry earth come morning. How long, we ask aloud. How long? And soon, when we feel that it is close, when the gale is just set to erode the last of our hill, and so to uncover those articles and acts and words and truths we were certain we had put deep enough that they would never again see daylight, we will button our coats and step over the threshold. We will leave our battered house behind and we will lean into that wind, making for the exposure of the baldest patch of land, where we will throw wide our arms and, like scraps of paper, hope to be carried away.

DOROTHY

My little girl is a bit timid. She routinely stands open-faced and mute when there are other people nearby. Observing. She's especially daunted in the presence of other children, older ones most of all. She eyes them zoologically, stands stock still as though afraid any movement will frighten them off, or alert them to her presence. I like to believe this is the reason that she's never shown off her ability to others, or even outside our house.

She's two-and-a-half years old, and she is something. I know it's my parental duty to say such things, and I know your place is to smile approvingly, then roll your eyes and shake your head once I look the other way. But you need to trust me on this: she really is amazing.

She asks me to sing her the alphabet song, and I'll do it but stop periodically at different spots, and she will, without hesitation, fill in the next letter. Two years old.

I hum the theme to *Sesame Street* to her and she breaks into song, getting most of the words right. Those she forgets she'll simply leave out, or she'll look at me with a great big open expression on her face, asking me to fill them in.

I know you're expecting a work of fiction. My name is

Andrew Forbes and I am a writer and a stay-at-home dad. I write short stories. Almost everything I write is fictional, but please trust me on this: this is a true story.

Dorothy, my wife Marie, and I live in Peterborough, Ontario. Marie writes policy concerning wildlife for the provincial government. Dorothy and I keep a very full schedule of playgroups, story circles at the library, gymnastics for toddlers, swimming lessons, and assorted errands. Our days are packed.

The girl loves animals, especially cats and dogs. We have an unruly blue heeler named Rebus and an odd-eyed white cat named Rudy. Dorothy laughs hysterically when the pets do the slightest thing, and nearly hyperventilates when the dog chases the cat. It's an unhinged, full-body laugh that we try to replicate with antics and tickling, but it never reaches the frenzied pitch it does when animals are involved.

And then there's this: Dorothy can walk up the wall and across the ceiling.

This is true.

She'll be standing on the wall so that she is sideways and you're straight up and down, and if she's holding a toy she'll drop it and it will fall hard onto our blond hardwood floors. She began doing this just before her second birthday, though she'd been walking on the horizontal plane since she was eleven months old.

We were in the family room, surrounded by toys. Marie was in the kitchen making herself a cup of tea. I think it was a Saturday morning. Dorothy lay on her side, pressed her feet to the wall just above the baseboards, and began walking. Soon she was halfway up the wall, giggling a bit. To Marie I said, "Look at this." Marie looked, slowly put down her mug, and walked toward us. "Be careful, Dot," she said.

"This is strange, right?"

"Well, yes," said Marie, but even without her saying so I could tell that she felt as I did: that all parents suspect their children to be exceptional, but here was our proof.

In a minute Dorothy had had enough, and simply walked back down to the floor.

"How did you do that, Dottie?" I asked.

"Oh, Dad, it's okay," she said.

"Dorothy," I said, "what's happening?"

"Daddy," she said, "I want a juice box." We still call them juice boxes, even though most of them are now little foil pouches.

Life is composed of things not said, or uttered once and never again. Odd as it seems, Dorothy's wall-walking quickly became just another facet of who we are as a family. People's days are full of special circumstances, of peculiar details. What takes place within the walls of our home is unique, as is what happens in yours. We have a familial understanding, a list of tics, things relayed almost telepathically. With a narrowed eye my wife can communicate to me what it would take you several paragraphs to make me understand. Her shoulders—the set of them, the tension held there—tell me everything I need to know about her mood, though it took me several years to learn to read them.

"What's wrong?" I'll say.

"How'd you know?"

"Your shoulders."

Likewise, with our children, we invent normalcy, craft anew the small stuff of daily life. This is what we've done with Dorothy: designed, or fallen into, our own kind of normal, though it may not resemble even remotely what happens around your kitchen table. Maybe your kid can recite the names of the prime ministers. Maybe you're expected to prompt him at every meal ("And after Borden?"). Maybe you cut the crusts off her toast without being asked. You know your children.

My daughter is articulate, musical, curious, and has somehow found the ability to defy gravity. We, as a family, have adapted and accommodated, and we'll continue to do so.

Some days, I'll admit, I just can't unearth the patience to humour her adventurousness. We'll all have breakfast, then Marie will leave for work, and I'll turn to my daughter and say, "Please, Dottie, no walking up the wall today, okay?" And she, brandishing the unblinking logic of a two-year-old, will say, "No, Daddy, I can walk on the wall because I can walk on the wall." How do you argue with that?

I should hasten to note that she is not universally amazing. She can't dress herself. The tantrums have become more severe lately, and she is brought out of them with ever greater difficulty. She can be rough with the cat. When she tires of a meal or a snack she's likely to just drop the remaining food on the floor. And, maybe most frustratingly of all, she's among the last of her friends to resist potty training. In a shameful turn we have resorted to bribery. If she uses, or even attempts to use, the potty, she gets one sticker in her notebook. We bought sheet after sheet of cows, horses, fairies, stars, moons, at the dollar store, anticipating buy-in on her part. So far, though, the sticker sheets are almost wholly intact. The notebook is mostly empty.

We are, I believe, conscientious parents. We read books and magazines about child-rearing. We go to the public library every week and we check out books about how to shepherd a toddler from diapers, through training pants, and on into the promised land of underwear worn confidently and without mishap. All of the literature—and there is a lot of literature—says that accidents are to be expected, steps backward, regressions, setbacks, and that we are not to make a big deal of them. But none of the books we have consulted mention how best to react if your child is standing on the bathroom ceiling, her ultra-fine blonde hair hanging down and brushing your face as you peer up at her, you imploring her to come down and try the potty just one more time, while she holds her training pants in her hand, waves them like a pennant, and then pees all over herself, and you, and the floor, while grinning.

Some nights I lie awake and dream up ways to harness her mysterious ability. "Dottie, can you dust the top shelf?" Window cleaning. Straightening pictures. I stand six-foot-three, and just as I have been asked time and again by stooped old women to retrieve items from high grocery shelves, so too will she wear the mantle of her gift. Into these things we are born.

Sometimes I tell Marie that we should take Dorothy to the climbing gym, where they have a fifty-foot wall studded with those little fake rocks. "It would blow their minds," I say. "No," she says, arms folded. "We should have fun with this," I say, but she reminds me that our daughter, our beloved first born, our only child, is not a circus freak. I concede the point while filing away a secret plan to buy Dottie a Spider-Man costume for Halloween.

On a bright Sunday, Dorothy and I were sitting at the dining room table. It was mid-afternoon, snack time. She sat on her knees on a chair. Before her was a plate with maybe a dozen red grapes, cut in half, three or four slices of cheddar, and a pile of Goldfish crackers. Outside the large picture window the wind blew errant snow flurries through the boughs of a pine.

"Dottie," I said, "why are you throwing things? Please stop throwing things." She had been tossing toys and food all day. She'd take them into her tiny hands, scamper up to the ceiling, then disperse them like a sprinkler head. A maniacal, laughing sprinkler head. The dog was beside himself.

"No. I want to throw things," she said. "I like to throw them and I will throw them and it's okay."

"Dorothy, please." I tried to sound stern, though no amount of sternness has ever altered her behavior, at least not that I can remember. But any day now, I've long thought, she'll start to recognize my fatherly authority. "Dottie, I want you to stay down here, please, and I want you to stop throwing things."

A dazzling lack of success left me frustrated, but not wanting Dorothy to see me frustrated, I went upstairs to our bedroom. Marie was not there. Neither was she in the spare bedroom across the hall, Dottie's room, or the bathroom.

"Marie?" I called. Dorothy was by then throwing something edible. I could hear the dog's claws scuff against the floor as he jumped. She giggled loudly.

"Marie?" I made my way to the basement and checked the office down there, as well as the workshop. Finally I found my wife in the laundry room, sitting cross-legged atop the clothes dryer, reading the fourth book in a series about a dystopic future populated by attractive teenagers. It must have been eight hundred pages long.

I asked, "Are you really hiding out down here, reading?"

"Yes," she said without looking up.

"That's a pretty good idea."

"I thought so." She had bought the book at an airport the week before, and she was by this time three-quarters of the way through it.

"She's throwing things," I said.

"I heard."

"What do I do?"

"Ignore her, maybe?" This is Marie's stock response, and the tactic has merit, if what you're hoping to do is downplay certain behaviour and refuse the one thing—attention—that a child hopes to gain by acting out. But in other cases, of course, it's a flawed technique, and with each shriek, each dog leap, each morsel of food raining downward, I felt a terrific anxiety and a great certainty that ignoring was not our best move here.

"I'd really like her to stop," I said, a new tide of frustration rising in my chest.

We were silent a moment, her atop the dryer, me leaning against the chest freezer. Upstairs Dorothy was still giggling, Rebus still desperately pouncing on whatever she was throwing (smart money was on the Goldfish crackers) and, because I know my dog, I'd bet his shoulders and back were hunched in a way which suggested that he knew what he was doing was "bad." It's a thing most dogs do, an instinctual display of deference, but in Rebus's case I like to imagine it's guilt, and that it's something he's learned from me.

I have a special talent for guilt, a knack, and in addition to the dog I believe also that I have taught Marie some of what I know, and I trust that Dorothy will inherit this, too. Guilt and an attendant suspicion of free time. Haunted by the thought: Shouldn't I be making myself useful?

I figure that somewhere along the line this is what became of the Protestant work ethic, warped, morphed, diluted over time. Marie is Catholic by birth, but lapsed enough that she has forgotten the precise mechanism of confession, that periodic tabulation and absolution. This has rendered her ripe for my lessons.

We pine for downtime but then regret it when it lands in our laps. We rent movies and return them unwatched.

But in one sense having a child like Dorothy has allowed me a measure of peace, of reduced expectations for myself. It has incrementally alleviated my guilt. The reasoning, however tortured, goes like this: if I do nothing else from here on out, I will still have had a hand in giving the world a wondrous human being, one worthy of scientific study. And there's also the hopeful thought, however dim, that this ability of hers is something I have passed on to her, some super ability that I never discovered and which fear now keeps me from exercising, but which nonetheless lies dormant in my makeup.

By the time I left Marie sitting atop the dryer and made my way up the stairs and toward the dining room, the commotion had stopped. Dorothy and Rebus were not in the dining room, but rather in the living room. He was curled up on the couch, asleep, and Dottie was sitting next to him, a picture book in her lap. She was looking at the illustrations and telling herself the story as she remembered it. The two of them there were quiet and still, and so like perfect angels—the dog's eyes closed, his chin resting near her knee, both of their faces relaxed, their postures soft and unthreatening—that I more or less forgot what had me so upset.

There is a photograph which shows Marie and me at Navy Pier in Chicago. Marie is six months pregnant, her face soft and cherubic. We are in Chicago as a grand kiss-off to our pre-parental life. Over an extended weekend we have seen the Cubs lose to Milwaukee, strolled the halls of the Art Institute, taken the El, roamed around the Loop, and seen the dolphin show at the aquarium. Now it is Sunday evening, the night before we are to fly home, and we are on Navy Pier, a questioning finger stuck outward into Lake Michigan, taking in the sights before retiring to a dark restaurant for deep dish pizza. The sun is sinking behind the skyline, and we are pausing for a photo, the camera in my hand at the end of my outstretched arm, pointed back at us. Her arms are around my waist, my left arm is over her shoulders. In the photo the lake appears as an indistinct bluish haze. There is a lighthouse tower at the end of the pier, just visible over Marie's shoulder. We are smiling, happy. And as I look at this photo now, it seems to me, with the wisdom bestowed by the intervening years, that if we resemble anything it is those seamen awaiting commencement of an atomic test at Bikini Atoll. We have been told time and again, by countless experts, some of what we might expect, but if we listened at all we did so blithely, casually, unable to absorb the enormity of it. But soon the thing will come, and it will be huge. And we are destined to live with its effects—the shockwaves and the lingering consequences. There will be no way to imagine our lives as they were before the event.

One night, recently, I was home alone with Dorothy when the power went out. It was a Thursday night and Marie was away on business, up north in Timmins, talking to a room full of hunters about moose and how many they should be allowed to shoot. She was due home that night. Dottie and I had just spent an hour on the couch reading storybooks and I was about to cook her some pasta, with olives and capers and heaps of Parmesan cheese, her favourite dinner. But before I could put on a pot of water the lights went out and the house fell silent, and that hum, the thing below and around us which is imperceptible except in its absence, was suddenly gone. Late February, already dark outside; my spirits sank. I went to the cupboard for candles, then found the flashlights. I fed Dorothy cold ham and tomato slices from the fridge and I made myself a ham sandwich. There were five tealights on the table and two pillar candles on the counter. They cast flickering circles of orangey light on the ceiling. Just as I was finishing my sandwich Dorothy grew bored with the remnants of her dinner, dismounted her chair, and began to walk up the wall behind me.

"Dottie, no," I pleaded. My heart felt as though it too had lost power.

"Yeah, yeah, yeah, yeah," she said excitedly, and in a moment she was on the ceiling, dancing around in the eddies of candlelight, clapping, laughing demonically. I hung my head in my hands, wondered if there was a chance that my child was the devil. With the tiny flames only barely cutting the darkness it seemed halfway possible, and it was too much for me on this shitty, powerless Thursday night in February. Damn me, I thought, and I began to weep. Dorothy sang fragments of the *Sesame Street* theme.

In time I managed to get her down—or rather, once she'd tired of shredding my nerves she decided to join me on the conventional plane. Soon power was restored, and I got her to sleep without further heartache. When Marie arrived home around 11:30 I was already four beers in and well on my way to getting decently drunk. A bad idea, I grant you, when you're home alone with a dependent, but since we live just a couple of blocks from the hospital

I felt like I was playing the odds. Marie, who'd flown from Timmins to Toronto and then taken a coach from there to Peterborough, decided to join me in my diminished state, so I went to the garage for a couple more bottles.

"How was your day?" she asked.

"Ah, you know," I said.

"Yeah," she said, twisting the cap, "I know."

And now, days later, as I sit writing this in my basement office—a dark, cozy room stuffed floor to ceiling with books, baseball souvenirs, and jazz records—the two great loves of my life are upstairs, the one trying to coax the other to sleep. It's quiet, which suggests success. No howls of protest filter down my way, no frantic footsteps, vertical or otherwise. Peace settles over our modest house, and our little handful drifts in a sea of dreams. And I have a moment to wonder: Is it simply the intensity of our love for Dorothy which raises her above the earth? Because we ask the same question that all parents ask: *Surely it can't be possible to love a child more?* So have we loved so hard that we have created a force capable of lifting her delicate frame even as no hands touch her? Then my wondering brings me someplace darker, as I tend to go, and I come to this: What if we have another child, a little sister or brother for our wunderkind, and that child turns out to be normal, unremarkable in that he or she is, like us, completely bound by gravity's pull? Could we find it in ourselves to overlook that? Would we love that child as much as we love Dorothy?

A STUNT LIKE THAT

My mother worked at Sears with a woman named Deb Schenkel. They sold appliances. Deb Schenkel smoked and she had a son, Glen, who smoked too. I mention this because my parents saw it as a kind of class division—people who smoked, people who didn't. They didn't.

It's hard to make friends as an adult, and usually not worth the trouble. My father understood that. My mother, though, would try, again and again. She set her sights on Deb Schenkel, though I couldn't tell you why, or what made Mom think that could work. I think Deb probably used to be pretty—you could still kind of see it—but then her husband left and she was stuck raising Glen and everything kind of went to hell. Mom must have felt sorry for her.

This was right around the time I wrecked my bike. I'd begged my folks for a red BMX, saved my paper route money and birthday cash, and they finally agreed to chip in to get the thing. I spent most of that summer going up to Steve Grienke's parents' cottage, an hour up the river. Jason, Steve's older brother, could drive, so we'd throw our bikes in the back of his big brown van and head up there. We'd drink beer and ride our bikes off a ramp and flip into the water.

So this one time I took off funny from the ramp and landed sideways, and the force of it twisted the handlebars and pulled the chain off. We decided the bike was worthless then, so we wrecked it. Swung it around and bashed it off trees, soaked the seat in lighter fluid and lit it up, slashed the tires with a hunting knife. It was one of those things you do when you're fifteen and it's summer and you're a little drunk before lunch.

"What in the hell were you thinking?" my father asked me. "I'm serious. List for me the thoughts that were running through your head."

"Their brains don't work the way ours do. I'm not saying this for effect," my mother said. "It's the truth."

"You'll excuse me if I have trouble with that," Dad said.

They said all of this right in front of me, like I wasn't even there.

I was their only child, of course, so they needed to believe that I'd only been following the lead of the evil Grienke brothers. If I only had better friends, I'd stay on the straight and narrow. That, I think, is part of why Mom pushed so hard on the Deb thing. She thought she and Dad would have someone to drink spritzers with, and I'd have Glen.

At school Glen was usually alone in the corner of the soccer field, eating lunch from a paper bag. Once I saw him having a boat race with twigs. I hadn't seen anybody do that since grade school. He was the kind of kid you figured liked to hurt animals.

Mom said, "Glen seems nice, doesn't he?" We were having Tuesday spaghetti, me, Mom, Dad.

"I guess," I said. "I don't really know him."

"His interests seem..." she said, "diverse."

"I don't know, he seems a bit weird, if you ask me," said

Dad, then looked at me. I wanted to laugh but didn't want him to know I agreed with him about anything, so I just twirled some more noodles onto my fork.

"I don't think that's fair, honey," she said.

"Weird or not, if he doesn't wreck your bike, I say go for it. New best friend," said Dad, his gold Century 21 blazer draped over the back of his chair.

My mother smiled at me. "It's good to make friends."

They dragged me over there one Sunday afternoon in June. Their whole house smelled like cigarette smoke. Summer was heating up and Deb had just had their in-ground opened up, so I was told to bring my trunks. I hated that: *trunks*. I said, "I'll bring my bathing suit."

Glen came upstairs. He said, "Hey."

I said, "Hey."

He asked me if I wanted to watch some movies.

"I don't know," I said. "I guess."

We headed downstairs and I could see by my Mom's face that as far as she was concerned Glen and I had just become best friends. She was kind of glowing.

Glen had a stack of gun magazines on his bedside table in his basement bedroom. It was always dark down there. There was a poster of cars, a Soviet tank, and three blonde women in ridiculous swimsuits. He had a VCR, too, and his video stash included action movies, motocross crashes, and a half a dozen porno tapes he'd stolen from one of Deb's ex-boyfriends.

We watched *Cyborg*, which was pretty bad. I didn't get the whole story because Glen kept fast-forwarding to "the fight parts."

"They need to get to Atlanta, but everybody's trying

to kill them," he said, trying to sketch the plot for me, remote in hand, scanning the tape. It didn't make much sense to me.

"There's a part where you can see the main girl's tits, too," he said.

"Really?" I said, maybe a bit too quickly.

He talked a lot about guns, and said he'd stolen the *Cyborg* tape from Zellers. He knew martial arts, and could kill a man with one kick.

"No way," I said.

He was wearing camouflaged pants and a red T-shirt with a yellow Ferrari on it. He had another T-shirt, black, with a fighter jet, and a blue sweatshirt. That was all I ever saw him wear.

The poolside party raged upstairs. My parents had brought over a jug of wine and Deb made it into sangria. They polished that off and Dad told some dirty jokes before passing out. Mom drove us home.

Not long after that they took Deb out to an Italian place. The plan was to leave me at the Schenkels' with Glen, which made no sense to me. Who was in charge? Two fifteen-year-olds do not equal one adult. I had the sense that something fucked up was going to happen.

As Dad swung the Topaz into Deb's driveway, Mom said, "This'll be great. You and Glen will have a chance to play." I was thinking, when you're fifteen you don't *play*, you *hang out*.

Deb opened the door wearing a black crocheted top, underneath which you could clearly see her black bra and pale torso. Tight black pants, and patent heels, big hair, hoop earrings. I was like, Wow. Dad reacted like that, too. He shot me a look behind Mom's back.

"Hello, Deb," Mom said.

"Let yourselves in," Deb said through the screen door. "I can't touch anything. My nails are drying." She flapped her hands and then blew on her nails. "Glen's in his room if you want to go down, Marky."

What do you say to that? What I said was: "Alright."

They left, saying they'd be back no later than ten (Mom), and don't do anything stupid (Dad), and there was some pop in the fridge and chips in the cupboard (Deb).

"Have fun," they all said.

We went swimming, which was fine. Glen did cannon-balls off the top of the slide. I kept waiting for him to brain himself on the deck, but no luck. We ate chips and called it dinner before watching *Cyborg* again. Glen showed me the scrambled pay-TV stations that showed softcore movies on Saturday nights. We watched the wavy screen for a while and listened to the dialogue. I thought I saw a nipple at one point. The music was really bad, and then the moaning started. I didn't know the first thing about sex, but it sounded fake.

"That's exactly how I'd give it to her," Glen said.

"For sure."

"Want to listen to some music?"

"Okay."

He put on a tape by Ministry. "This fucking rules," he said. He danced a bit, stomping around in a circle, pumping his fists. He looked stupid, but seemed happy. I was embarrassed, and I think maybe that was because I knew I couldn't do what he was doing. Glen turned off the overhead light and switched on a lamp with a red bulb in it.

"What do you want to do now?" he asked.

"Don't know. Listen to more music?"

He put on Pigface and turned it up too loud.

"Check this out," he shouted, and then pulled his cock out of his pants. "Let's see yours." I hesitated, because it was weird. But I guess I figured what the hell. Or maybe I figured it would be more weird not to do it, if that makes sense. Finally I said to myself, Who would he tell? He didn't talk to anybody at school. So I pulled mine out, and they both dangled there, about the same size, limp, veiny as shrimp. He stared at mine. I stared at his.

"Can you make it hard?" he asked.

"I don't know," I said. "Maybe."

We lay on our backs on the cold linoleum floor of his basement bedroom side-by-side. Our penises flopped out of our pants. We talked about what we'd like to do with them, and who we wished would touch them. We passed an hour that way. The red light burned into my eyes and the music throbbed. Then Glen grabbed himself and I worried that he was about to try something, but he just tucked his dick back into his pants, zipped, and stood up.

"You wanna smoke?"

"I guess," I said, and I put myself away and followed him upstairs into Deb's bedroom. He dug a pack out of her top drawer, where I could see black lace things.

"Emergency stash," he said. We went up onto the roof, out the bathroom window and onto the warm shingles.

"Watch this," he said, then walked to the corner of the roof and started pissing over the side. I could see the arc disappearing into the night, hear it ringing off the rocks in the garden below.

We were smoking on the roof when they arrived. I don't know why we didn't try to duck inside as the car came around the corner. I heard it and felt dead certain it was theirs. But I took my cues from Glen and he didn't move, he just kept smoking. In that moment I thought, He's not afraid of his mother. And I wondered what that would feel like, to be beyond their reach.

As we drove home my father said to me, "Smoking, Mark? Of all the stupid things." Then he said: "If you ever pull a stunt like that again, you'll be out on your duff so fast."

Then we were quiet. I just kept thinking that if Dad knew all of it, about Glen's dick, that I'd shown mine, he'd kill me right there. But I felt worse for my mother, who sat quietly in the front seat looking at the dashboard. I knew my parents wouldn't be seeing Deb Schenkel anymore. I thought that was a sad thing, because maybe they'd have turned out to be good friends. And I hated to think I'd ruined that.

It was about a year later that Mom died of the pancreatic cancer she would've already had that night. My father became unreachable. He stopped talking to me for a while, nothing beyond "Hello" and "Go to bed."

At the funeral I started thinking of Glen, for some reason. Neither he nor Deb were there, but I remembered the way my mother looked that night in the front seat of the car. Her shoulders were slumped and her head bowed. It made me sad to picture her in a brown pleather coat, the glow of streetlights moving by. It still makes me sad to remember, to imagine what she must have been feeling. Then—you know how your mind runs away on you—I started picturing Glen's pecker. And right away I said to myself: What a terrible thing to think about at your mother's funeral.

THE MARYS

Mary 7 wakes us with bad news. Someone's at the perimeter, she says. I think it's them.

You rehearse and you rehearse and then the real thing is upon you. I jump from the bed and run to check the CCTV on the laptop in the kitchen. There's something there, along the northern fence and at the east gate. Smudges upon the small screen, but most definitely them. Dark, menacing shadows. I switch to the night vision but it isn't working. There is interference.

I had always expected them to come from the sky.

Here we go, I say. The trials are upon us, I say. You all know what to do. We snap to with a military precision. I indulge in a moment of pride over what I have wrought. Such order amid chaos.

The children above the age of five all know their roles. Most of them look like me. The boys generally get my proud chin, the girls my cheekbones, steely eyes. They are clean and their clothes are neat. They are respectful and demure. Well-raised children. I will be careful here not to take too much credit; I let the women take care of most of the caregiving. This isn't some Old Testament doctrinal thing on my part, more a matter of knowing what you're good at and what you aren't.

In the first few moments of action my wives all move to their stations. For each person here there is a station, a responsibility, an area of expertise that they are expected to know backward and forward, a thing they are ready to die for, if it should prove necessary. An example being Mary 7, my newest wife. She keeps the dogs, trains them, feeds them. In a situation such as this it will be her responsibility to know how long to keep them penned, and when it will be time to release them to their fate, their gnashing teeth in search of waiting flesh on their way down to hell.

The younger children are herded toward the secure nursery. On his way by, Mary 4's youngest stops at my feet and tugs on my pant leg. Hi, he says, stretching his arm up. This means high five. He wants a high five. I smile and hold my hand just above his curly-haired head and let him slap my palm. Yay, he says, then falls back in line. The boy is sweet but has a cruel streak in him that makes me wish you could arm a two-year-old. He'd protect us all, I'm sure of it. He's never as attentive as when he's watching some of the other children at their video games. We have five Xbox consoles, but I only let them play the shooter games. Somebody told me the US Army uses them for training. Well if they don't they should, I said.

The first Mary would have been the only and the last, had she stayed. That woman had all a man desires and requires, save devotion, apparently. Save belief. But there was enough good in her, enough of a mix of the earthly and the potentially divine to linger with a man until his dying day and then beyond. I met the second Mary a day after the original left, in line at the Safeway, and her eyes told me she needed something to cling to. Come with me, I said, and she did. Shorter than the first Mary, sturdy but not stocky. She bore me my second and third sons. Her family came sniffing but she herself told them there was no place for them here.

At night, beneath these trees, at the edge of this plain, when the insects begin their chorus and the wind combs the fields, I think I will miss this life, this iteration of reality. When I have my choice of wives to lie with, next to an open window, and the children are safely tucked up, and that night's wife gives herself over to me.

But then I have only to consider what awaits us in the next epoch, and I am recommitted to the exercise, to the process.

I have something which cannot be called fear, perhaps trepidation, in a small recess next to my stomach. I can feel it there, hard and round. I mustn't allow it to dissuade me, of course, but it is there. Out by the bigger of the two Quonsets my horse Meshach stirs. I consider, for a brief, cowardly moment, mounting him and riding across the prairie and leaving all this, all which is soon to pass. I could make for a city—Saskatoon, perhaps. There I could preach at the eleventh hour about the perils to come, the nature of the Rapture and the path through Hell to the paradise which awaits.

But that isn't my role, of course. My preaching is done. This is where I am needed now, required to act my part as the very tip of a great and faithful arrow aimed at the heart of the awful world-swallowing beast. Here and now. This is the moment and these are the chosen and I am their leader. The Quonset, which sits like a hunched steel animal with its back turned on the world, houses much of our arsenal, and three of my eldest boys are headed there now to fetch the sacks which contain the assault rifles. I scan the sky and see nothing but the early hint of morning. Okay, I think, you devious SOBs, for they are devious, Come at us. Come and attempt to inflict your worst. I am expecting ominous beings, misshapen, malformed, something this world could not dream up, but if they wish to come in the form of a Mountie detachment from Lloydminster, that's their business and who are we to say.

I ask Mary 5, who is securing the nursery door, if she checked the wiring on the charges at the east gate this week, as she is to do every week. You know I did, she says.

Mary 3, who I always thought looked a lot like Grace Kelly, if Grace Kelly were shorter and more a kind of dirty blonde, is standing in the middle of the room, looking at the floor. What is she looking for? I laid with her last night. Is she the last woman I will know carnally? Did we succeed in planting another seed? What are you looking for, Mary? I ask.

My sock, she says. Have you seen my other sock?

Your sock?

It's cold in here, she says. She is wearing a khaki work shirt and one red sock. Nothing covers her legs, but she holds a pair of Levi's by a belt loop. I don't ask that they wear bonnets and ankle-length dresses. That'd be weird. Practical clothes, jeans mostly. Work wear, for there is always more work to be done.

I haven't seen it, I say. But there's a basket of clean laundry in the closet. Find another pair. Then get your weapon. As I am saying this I am hoping that Mary 2 is not within earshot. She's kind of a zealot when it comes to the laundry being put away. Mary 3 rubs her eyes. Alright, alright, she says.

I stand with my shoulder to the wall and peek out the window, to the southeast. A pinkish light blushes the horizon and against it I see two of my oil derricks nodding as though in deference to something great and terrible. It used to be that every time those derricks bobbed I saw dollar signs. Now their motion in the corner of my eye causes my heart to skip a beat. Every movement might be an agent of our enemy racing to a new position, a better place from which to spy us, and to fire upon us.

In reality of course there is no sense in trying to mask our movements, because whatever we do, they see. They see and they know. When we defecate. When we make love. When the milk in our refrigerator is past its date. The awful things we find ourselves up against have ways we cannot comprehend. We can only adapt.

Are Adam and them back with the duffel bags yet? I ask. Mary 3 says, Not yet I think. I go through the doorway and back into the kitchen to check the CCTV. There are cars on the approach road, three that I can make out, and I see Adam and Mark and Matthew laden with bags, the guns, coming to the back door of this bungalow.

It is getting lighter by the moment and this gives me tension, for I suspect they want to launch their assault before daylight. Or perhaps they want us to see them, their terrible forms, before they spread darkness across the Earth and black out the sun, before they gouge out a few billion sets of eyes with their terrible claws.

Perhaps all of it means nothing to them. I consider this. Perhaps this gives them no more pause than filling a gas tank or cleaning a firearm would cause me to stop and think over what I am doing. Perhaps it is simply who they are, ignorant of malice, bred to do a thing and move on to the next world and do the same thing again, mindful not of the cries and the blood.

What will they look like? asks Mark.

We have no way of knowing, I tell him. Grotesque, ten-

tacled things? Small green men? We don't know. I have a
feeling they will look like normal men. That's the worst trick.

Oh, says he.

I say, Everything we have learnt is dwarfed by all we have
yet to learn. In the next few moments you will learn more
than you have known your entire life.

Mark, who is scrawny and delicate and brash, but who is
nevertheless an excellent shot, says nothing to this. Instead
he turns on the radio and we are all inundated with detest-
able dance music.

Taylor Swift, he says with a quick smile of recognition.

Find a news station, I tell him.

He begins turning the little wheel and when he finds the
public broadcaster's station they are carrying on as per usual.
Nothing happening in the rest of the world, says Adam.

Fool, I say, don't you think that's what they want us to
believe?

Mary 7 comes in the house and says the dogs are all
penned up. They're agitated, she says. They ought to be, I
say. In her I see such tenderness. She is two months along
now. Her features are just beginning to soften. I have placed
her on an ultra-high-calorie diet because in a dream I saw
that she is carrying twins.

The first Mary was a twin. Her sister was a teacher in
Toronto, that stinking pit. I think that's where she went, to
be with her sister. When I first told her about what was to
come she asked me when we would bring our families here
to be with us, to be protected. I said no family. This is your
family. She wavered then, the first such instance. We sat in
wire lawn chairs next to a fire I'd built in an old truck rim.
The air was chilled. This was probably May or early June, so
many years ago. Mary's soft brown hair caught the firelight

and her skin was clear and white. Her eyes narrowed. But my family is who I am, she said. I know who you are, Mary, I said. You are me. You are this, my arm sweeping around to indicate the land, and this, I said, putting my hand on my heart. Of course, she said, and she knelt in front of me, rested her head in my lap. I believe very firmly that we became pregnant that night with Adam, my first son. Such a woman. I'd have filled her with so many beautiful children, had she possessed the fortitude to see this through.

The radio is still talking and the lights still burning when the power is cut. I expected this; the electromagnetic radiation from their crafts. In a heartbeat the backup generator kicks in. I can hear its diesel engine fire to life out there, out by the second house. Then it too fails, and there is silence. Just the wind. A faint pinkish light from the windows. I see shadows all around me. The boys, young men now, with proud chests, shoulders back, chins up. I see my wives' faces, faintly, and they are smiling because they know where we will soon be. The youngest children are all tucked away in the secure basement nursery. Though I can hear nothing, see very little, I know that out there on the prairie, silent machinations are underway to finally bring this thing to a head. We are on the precipice here. What's coming is unlike anything any human being has ever known.

People ask me do I really believe this stuff. I tell them that I live it and I breathe it and I know it to be true. There is no question of mere belief. Ask me that question tomorrow, when the whole of the Earth is scorched black and the cities have fallen and your family is all gone. When the crops are burnt, the oceans dry, and gashes to dwarf the Grand Canyon have been opened upon the land. When most all mankind has finally been called to task but me and mine are still here, still fighting. Ask me then do I believe. And I will ask you, do you finally believe? And who is so crazy now?

I am not given to sentimental thoughts, especially not now, not as I bring the Kalashnikov to my shoulder and lean in to line up the first shot. I am not wistful and I am not fooled by this world's illusions, but some recessed part of me can't help but spare a thought for the first Mary, fallen and sullied though she is. It would be nice, after all, to know where she is, who she is with, and how she will fare in all this. I am thinking of her, of her eyes, and how she is the only person I would allow to come into this place, now. About how Adam can't even remember his own mother's face, and how I'd like for that to change, when their vehicles, a lot more vehicles than I'd figured, throw on their searchlights, bathing us all in a cold luminescence, casting hard shadows against the walls. It is with the first Mary in mind, then, that I use the Kalashnikov's barrel to break the brittle glass of the window, and begin to squeeze with the index finger of my shooting hand. Maybe, it occurs to me, as the walls begin to buckle and deflate and the crashing voices begin to call to us in their indecipherable tongues, maybe this might have gone differently if she hadn't left, my first beloved Mary.

THE GAMECHANGER

I'm all about Robert Grainge right now. His mother, Claudette, tells me on the phone it's pronounced "Ro-bare." She says, "Like the French."

"We'll put that in the media guide," I tell her, "so that everybody knows it's Ro-bare, not Robert." She likes that.

Ro-bare Grainge is my whole life right now. Me and every other major Division I basketball recruiter. He's the top scorer in the nation, a rangy guard with great handling and plus defence. He's six-five, and he loves the paint. Always knows where to find his teammates. A gamechanger. We watch tape of him while we eat our Corn Flakes. We read his stat sheet while lying in bed. He consumes us.

I want to put him with Dallas Carmody, a smooth shooting guard, a real perimeter guy from Indiana who the Hoosiers loved until I swooped in and poached him. I don't even know how I did it, to be honest. But I did, and he wears orange for us and he finished his freshman year the fourth-highest scorer in the country.

Carmody and Grainge is a combination of names that sweetens my dreams at night. I see Grainge in a backcourt with Carmody in two years' time. I see Grainge handling

and slashing into the key. I see him drawing bodies over—
because everybody fears Grainge—and I see him kicking
the ball out to Carmody. I see Carmody burying a long
jumper, or a three from the wing. I see this over and over
and over. I see KU falling. I see Duke falling. I see a tournament run. I see a title.

My office is a thousand high school gyms. My office is the
airport at 6:00 AM. My office is a housing development in
Youngstown, Ohio. My office is the IHOP on Route 16. My
office is the dome packed with thirty thousand people when
Georgetown visits. My office is the goaty-meaty-vinegary
smell of young men exerting themselves and the clatter
of a dozen dribbled balls in the practice gym. My office is
wherever they need it to be.

My wife, Pam, will call me on my phone and say, "Where
are you, Eddie?" I'll say, "Pine Bluff." I'll say, "Chicago." I'll say,
"In the driveway, Pammy." She'll ask how it went and I'll say, "I
think we've got this one," or "Hard to tell," or "His brother
went to Michigan and he's pretty set on going there too."

Sometimes I land these young men and sometimes I
don't, but if I don't there likely isn't anyone else who could
have. Believe that. Petey, or Dont'e, or Ellis, or LaShawn, or
David, had his mind made up before I landed on his doorstep, because his brother went somewhere else, or because
the Jayhawks just won a title and they have a spot at power
forward where he might get actual freshman minutes, or
because his friends always wore Carolina gear and now he
wants to wear the uniform, or whatever.

Sometimes they say no but I don't believe them, so I make
one more trip. What the hell; between the Athletic Director
and the alumni our budget is virtually bottomless. I've never

been told no, and my card has never been refused.

On too many occasions to count, such last-ditch trips have yielded fruit. No, they said, but I said, Hold on, let's talk about this a bit more. I said, Why don't I fly out there and we can have dinner, me and you and your dad, and we'll just be sure you're making the right choice.

And come signing day in April, what was the address on those letters of intent?

Right now, there is only one letter I'm interested in seeing. The wait breeds a restlessness in me I can't stand, so I've decided to come see Grainge play again, and maybe put the bug in his ear once more. I've made the trip for this weekend high school tournament in December, braving the three-plus-hour drive down I-81 from upstate to the rusted heart of Pennsylvania. Christmas has come and gone but the new year is not yet upon us. The days are cold.

Technically we have until April, but these winter days are where this battle is lost or won. I've seen recruiters from other schools make the mistake of hanging back for too long, losing their player. You have to become a part of the kid's life. You have to become a part of his emotional landscape. Fill him with good feelings and stories of glory and potential victory so rich with detail that they function like memory. Start early. Make him see it. Let him feel it. Tell him, "You, in orange, cutting down that net at the end of the tournament." Repeat times a million. Get right inside his head, between the thoughts of girls and the lyrics of songs and the early memories of basketball on TV.

You have to do the legwork. Spend the fall and winter in regional airports and in rental cars and gyms and arenas. In chain restaurants and shitty motels. The Nite Owl. Super 8. Sandy's Sleep Inn. The Comfort Inn, within sight of the mighty Susquehanna River, in Harrisburg, PA.

In desperate cases it might be necessary to call in the coach. Insist that he fly out and get a rental car and arrive on the kid's doorstep to make his impassioned pitch. And yes, to anticipate the question, Grainge is a desperate case. Accordingly, Coach B is due here in a few weeks. I didn't think that would be necessary, but no one's heard one way or the other from Robert, and this makes me anxious, makes us anxious. Such anxiety is the sort of thing that requires me to visit exotic locales like wintry Harrisburg.

In December this part of the world is the colour of ash— the ground, the light, the sky. My car is white. It disappears. Late last night, when I got in, I parked beneath a light stanchion in the Comfort's lot but this morning I couldn't tell which light it'd been. I had a strange moment of disorientation as I walked around that lunar landscape and couldn't quite recall just where I was, let alone where I'd left my car. Once that lifted and I had identified the white hump beneath the white mound of snow, I brushed and scraped and warmed it up, then made for a face-to-face with Don Sykes, Grainge's coach at Harrisburg High.

I meant to pump Sykes for indications as to which way Robert might be leaning, under the guise of asking about the kid's development since I'd last watched him play, back in September.

"What more can I tell you?" Sykes told me, leaning back in his office chair and rubbing the white stubble atop his head. "Kid's ready. He's readier than ready."

"Good. I need to hear this, Don."

"Best I've seen, Eddie. And getting better."

"Okay. Good." But no indication as to which way Grainge is leaning.

I spend the afternoon in my room, watching video, talking to my people back upstate. My room is quiet and dark, a cave of study and contemplation. A base of operations, an impermanent temple to the game.

It's basketball. It's always been basketball. The reason I can stand being away from Pam so often, stand the bad hotels and the terrible food. The reason, if you really want to drill down, that Pam and I are childless. It's an unreasonably demanding job, but I do it because it allows me be within this world, on hardwood courts, in old arenas, talking to men and boys about this game, all the time. My father took me to see Oscar Robertson and the old Cincinnati Royals when I was six years old, and that was it. There was no turning back from that. Since then I have seen Wilt, and Bill Russell, and Dr. J. I've seen Magic and Bird and Jordan. I've seen LeBron. And I've loved every minute of it. I'm fortunate, as I see it, to get paid to float through this world, looking for the next great. I'm pulled by the hope that I might find him, but I'm sustained day in, day out by nothing more than this game. Dribble and pass and catch and shoot.

I've watched uncountable hours of video. Call it bearing witness. I have a ton to get through right now. We're kind of hitting a crunch time. Robert Grainge is not my only quarry, not by a long shot, but he's my top priority. My obsession, actually. I wind up watching a highlight reel of him three times in a row before I take a shower and head out to the gym to see the day's games.

"Orange Eddie!" someone bellows, and I wheel around to see Bill from Duke standing with his arms outstretched in surprise, or supplication, or greeting. "Haven't seen you at the Hilton," he says, and chuckles. Bill is short and round and red-faced. He makes liberal use of the agricultural product that once made North Carolina prosperous, and he has the deep-chest wheeze and yellowed teeth to show for it.

"It was booked up," I say. "I'm at the Comfort."

"Well, it's got colour cable TV and a bed, right? They're all the same."

"Sure," I say. "A place to sleep."

"Right, right."

"Grainge is ours," I say. "You don't have anywhere for him to play."

"Oh, we'll find somewhere," says Bill from Duke. "Talent like that, we'll find him room."

"It's not a good fit, Bill."

"You have this locked up, do you? Fine. I guess I'll head on home, then. That'll mean a vacancy at the Hilton, if you're quick."

"I look for a non-smoking room."

"Right, right. Look, Ed, I think this is going to be close. I sense that from him. I think you, me, and KU are in this. But in the end, you know, my guess is he'll opt for the program with the best chance of winning a title. And with respect," he smiles, "I think you know that's us. At least for the next few years."

"That's a lot to assume, Bill," I say. "I wouldn't concede that."

"Your frontcourt is weak, Ed."

"We expect some big improvement there."

"You're not talking to your boosters here, Ed. You can drop the Cinderella line."

"Have you seen him yet this weekend?"

"I have. Thirty-four and twelve last night, with eleven rebounds." He says "eleven" as though it were three separate words.

"I heard."

"He's something, Ed."

"That's why we're here, isn't it?"

Released from Bill's moist grip, I float through the corridors of Harrisburg High, making my way toward the gym. Everything else is quiet, dark, still. Hallways, classrooms. 4:00 PM and the light is abandoning central Pennsylvania, leaving us all to huddle in the warm electric glow of an aging brick high school. At the centre of it all thrums the heart, bright and overfull. People straggle and stream toward and away from the heavy double doors. I buy a ticket, two dollars—Proceeds to the Prom Committee—and push through the doors into the gym.

Banners, signs, boys and girls in sweatshirts, their faces painted. The aluminum bleachers are crowded but not full. Serious-looking men in fleece sweaters or windbreakers sit near the back, holding clipboards and tablet computers. I recognize a few of them. Mothers and sisters and fathers and brothers sit together, attempting to combine the force of their love and project it out to a certain boy, to make him able to do things he has never done before. They hope that their boy will do something remarkable or miraculous tonight, or this weekend, and so vault himself into the stratosphere of boys hunted by those men with their clipboards. A scholarship. A free ride.

I take a seat on the end of a row, three quarters of the way up. I'm not taking notes. I've done my homework. I've talked to Grainge's parents, talked to his coach, talked to his buddies, talked to the guy who covers high school sports for *The Patriot-News*. Talked to the folks from the scouting agencies. Talked to Coach B. Scanned numbers, pored over game notes. Most importantly, I've watched the kid play and I've asked myself: Does he look like a man among boys? Does he appear blessed with an extra set of skills and senses as compared to his teammates and opponents?

Sometimes one or more parts of this equation are out of line, or untrustworthy. I have seen kids who lit up scoreboards for four years but weren't even close to what we were looking for. I have heeded the alarm sounded by my instincts and passed on "can't-miss" players from good high school or prep programs, and then watched them trundle off to other high profile Div I teams only to flame out before their junior year. Bottom line, you have to watch the kid play. Your eyes will tell you whether it's a yes or a no.

With Robert Grainge, everything points to yes. My employers are convinced, and so am I. So now I'm just here to watch and, if the opportunity presents itself, to pitch again. I'm always prepared to pitch.

I scan the floor. The Harrisburg Cougars, in white, are playing a team from Altoona, the Lions, whose maroon uniforms are classically handsome. It takes me a moment to get acclimated to the game, to pick out the players and just what is going on. It's right before the half and the Cougars are up 34-28.

Things become still for the tiniest moment, and then there he is. Grainge—he'll need to hit the gym this summer—all limbs and joints. He stands in for a free throw. The world spins at his feet. Watching him, in the clamour of a banner-festooned gym, I'm giddy. It might be the hours I keep, but I feel carbonated, the happiness rising off me like bubbles, the sense that I'm exactly where I should be: watching Robert Grainge sink bucket after bucket on a Friday night in a brightly lit high school gym in Harrisburg, Pennsylvania.

Find me a kid who loves the fundamentals, that's what

I've always said. And Grainge is most definitely that kid, spending an hour on his free throws after practice, his dribbling drills, his picture-perfect passes. His drive to the basket off a screen is pure poetry.

I should say, too, that he is indeed capable of flash. I've seen him uncork it at practice, squaring up one-on-one against a teammate during down moments, and even after Sykes has released them to their lives. Grainge is versed in a collection of jukes and ghost moves that shake an opponent until dizzy. So he has those skills, but he eschews them during gameplay in favour of a sound, unspectacular, but incredibly effective style.

Frankly, I love him. He would be the absolute perfect fit for our team, for the culture of Do It Right that Coach B preaches, for the holes we're facing on next year's squad, for the campus, for the community—he's just perfect.

The Cougars win handily, and Grainge is the reason, putting in twenty-five with eight helpers and nine boards. Now another game is underway in the gym, but without the home squad to cheer for, or the prospect to see, the spectators have thinned. I have stuck around, riding a hunch that I might outlast the other recruiters, the ones who are still doing their homework. They'll head back to their hotel rooms and pore over their laptops, send an email update to the AD, then maybe hit the hotel bar.

I'm watching the doors, which I hope are the right doors, waiting for Grainge to emerge. He's taking his time.

Then he comes out. He's guileless—I saw it right away the first time I met him, and it's still true. All of this swirls around him, but he's just living his life. Being alive, with so few designs, so few notions of responsibility and obligation that he might as well be an infant. It heartens me to see. This boy has no screens.

"Hello, Robert," I say, extending my hand.

"Mr. Eddie," he says, and he seems genuinely, though shyly, happy to see me.

"Great game out there," I say.

"You watched?"

"Most of it, yes."

"Yeah, they were playing tight. Pretty aggressive. We had to move it around a lot."

"They were never in the game, Robert."

"Haw, I don't know. It was good to win."

I'm fifty-two years old, and it is my job to have conversations with teenage boys. It's an odd arrangement from most angles, and I am never less than aware of the differences between us. But Robert doesn't seem unhappy to be talking to me, just shy, as though he can't understand all the attention. I'm lucky he recognized me as soon as he did, to be honest; this boy's life is a whirlwind of middle-aged white men right now. He'd be forgiven for failing to match a name to a face, but the fact that he does fills me with hope that I have a real shot in this.

His phone chirps, a muffled half-verse of a rap song.

"Uh oh," I say. "Bet that's Bill from Duke."

He laughs, digs the phone from his hip pocket, and checks the screen. "Naw. My girlfriend." Without answering he slides the phone back into his jeans.

"Who's your girlfriend?"

"Monique."

"Monique. She nice?"

At this his face breaks wide open and his teeth explode out into the world, involuntarily. "Yeah," he says, and his eyes twinkle. "The nicest." He's disarmed. A sweet kid with no toughened hide to show the world. He'll have a hard time.

"You sure it wasn't Bill from Duke?"

"Positive. Besides, I'd never go to Duke. Hate those guys."

"Music to my ears," I say, and it is. "Play for us. You can beat Duke." I'm quiet, earnest. I can feel my eyes begin to shine. This is a crucial, naked moment. It is the sort of exchange that can make or break this thing. I need him to feel that I am open and honest and have nestled in my aging, crusty heart only the absolute best interests of everyone involved.

He smiles a deflecting smile. "Honestly? I'm worried about your defence," he says. "That's my concern."

"What is it about Coach B's defence that worries you?"

"You play that zone, that two-three."

"Almost always. Except when we press."

"Yeah, well, I have some skill on defence. You seen that."

"No question." I know just where this is going because I've heard it before.

"I hear that teams, when they're drafting, don't pick your guys too high because they feel like that defence doesn't get them ready for the pro game, for man-to-man. I want to play man, I want to get those steals, block some shots. I want those numbers. Feel like they'd up my draft position."

I smile, fold my hands together. "Where was Waiters picked?"

"Fourth."

"Carmelo?"

"Three," he says, and then that smile comes back, all the teeth. He starts to chuckle.

"What?"

"You know I love 'Melo," he says, "But the man can't defend."

"That's not the zone's fault," I say.

A wave of people—the last of the Harrisburg players, managers, hangers-on—emerges from the locker room doors and overtakes us. They bounce and laugh and I turn my head to watch them go, and that's when I see Marvin Grainge, father of Robert, swimming against their current and straight toward us. And I see immediately, in the disrupted air between his face and his son's, that I have tipped the apple cart, that Marvin is angry and Robert is guilty, presumably due to an understanding that, though we've had our share of talks, him and I, one-on-one, in bleachers, across tables, in locker rooms, the boy isn't to speak to the likes of me without his father present.

Marvin's a sturdy man, though in six feet of water he would need a straw to breathe. His youngest boy ended up in the position he's in now partly by fortunate natural fluke and partly because, in order to give his two sons every chance they might have, Marvin has driven a bus for twenty-two years, occasionally holding a second job as a custodian.

"Robert!" he barks. "Time to go. Come on, now. You know better than this. Do I have to write it on your arm, boy? So you don't forget?"

"Mr. Grainge," I say.

He looks at me, wiggles his full moustache, seems to need a moment to decide what to say. Finally he gives me a terse, "Goodnight to you, Mr. Eddie," and they are out the door, out into the ashen December night.

Some of them present themselves as men until a crack shows, a betrayal of their age. They'll get giddy over a new video game, or miss their mother so acutely that tears come over the breakfast buffet. Some of them assume silence is the best way to be taken seriously. They glower at you. "I let my game speak for me." I've heard more than one young man say these words. Others, like Robert Grainge, are so very obviously still boys that it nearly breaks my heart to pry them from the nest and drop them off a cliff in the hopes that they'll suddenly learn to fly.

But you also have to learn to let them surprise you. I assumed Dallas Carmody was an innocent hick, the sweet-faced, blond-headed son of a farm insurance salesman who said "ma'am" and "sir," soft blue eyes and ears like pitchers of milk. Then he told me about what crystal meth had done to the young population of his small Indiana town. "I've had two friends die, and I've known sixteen-year-old girls, pretty as you can imagine, who'd trick themselves out to the nastiest men alive. All my friends are screwed up," he said. "Get me the fuck out of here."

What you can't forget, no matter how composed or stoic or strong they appear, no matter how close to being ready for the pros, is that they are children. Sometimes you have to lie to them, and sometimes you have to stay up all night talking to them, and sometimes you have to bail them out of jail. You have to know that they will need their egos stroked, their chins wiped, their shoes tied. You have to remember that they will follow a girl across two upstate counties on a stolen bicycle the night before a nationally televised game against a top five team because he and the girl are "meant for each other." You have to remember that they will cry. You have to expect them to fail. And you have to know that someone has to be there to catch them.

My thinking? It might as well be us.

Back in my room, before my fatigue catches up with me, I snare Pam on the phone. She's awake, but barely. I can hear it in the corners of her voice.

"How'd today go?" she asks a bit distractedly.

"Oh, good. Yeah, okay."

"But no commitment."

"You can tell."

"You'd have told me by now, Ed."

"Yeah, I would have."

"Talk to him, at least?"

"Him and Grainge Senior, yes."

"Oh." The echo tells me she's in the kitchen, which means she's curling the long cord around her fingers. She does this without knowing she's doing it. We still have a corded phone in the kitchen, ivory-coloured, the cord long enough to walk from one end of the room to the other. Pam doesn't trust cordless phones, says they're always cutting out at inopportune times. When you're talking to your mother or your insurance agent. "The hard case," she says.

"The very one. Hustled Robert off before I could get my spiel out."

"Protective."

"Hostile, very nearly."

"Did you get to see him play, though?"

"Oh, he's something, Pammy. He's really something."

"The next big one?"

"I've really fallen for this one," I say.

"Remember rule number one, Eddie," she says. Then we sign off in our private language of memory and affection, the unique patter we've spent twenty-eight years inventing. I sleep like a log, and I'm near certain she does the same.

In the morning I grab a muffin and a coffee at the hotel's continental breakfast bar, take a chair at a wobbly table, watch a reel of sports highlights on the screen nearest my head. The Lakers look terrible. The Bulls are missing a wheel. The Knicks, as always, are ridiculous.

Saturday morning rolls on. The Harrisburg Invitational Tournament games start at ten o'clock and I have to tell you it's a lovely and novel thing to watch basketball so early in the day. By nine-thirty I am fed and caffeinated, looking for parking in the snowy HHS lot.

Inside, the dry electric heat induces a thick drowsiness in me. The day's first two teams are warming up on the court. The Cougars aren't one of them, but after a few minutes I spot Robert, head and shoulders above those around him, and next to him is a girl who must be Monique. They are laughing and needling one another. I don't want to interrupt, so I sit a few rows away.

After the buzzer sounds to end the first half, though, Robert stands and stretches, turns toward me. I don't mean to but I catch his eye, and he smiles, waves, and beckons me with one of his big hands. I stand and work my way toward him.

"Mr. Eddie, this is Monique," he says, and she puts out a smooth hand for me to shake.

"Mr. Eddie, nice to meet you. I've heard about you from Robert. You're the Duke man, right?"

There's a nervous chuckle. "Naw," Robert says, "He's the other one, baby."

"Oh, right, of course. Sorry. Nice to meet you, Mr. Eddie."

"Happy to meet you, Monique," I say. "And I've heard of you. Robert's eyes light up when he says your name."

"They better," she says, and gives him a mock-serious face. He chuckles.

"Robert," I say, "I wanted to apologize for last night. If I overstepped—"

"No sweat. That's just Dad," he says.

"He was riding you pretty hard," I say.

He shrugs his large, angular shoulders. "He's just trying to do what's best for me. I let it roll off," he says. It's a lie. He's been told he must be tough, he's seen it and been fed it since infancy. Some cloistered, pink, human part of me wants to tell him, *Don't get tough, don't get tough. Don't lose that openness. Hold tight to your wonder.*

But he can't, not if he's going to have any success at what he's chosen to pursue. Or been chosen to pursue. Most of us have just one thing we're truly good at, and we best serve the world by doing it. That was true long before Dr. Naismith ever hung his peach basket. But part of me wonders if Grainge's duty to his own tender humanity outweighs the responsibility he has to his wondrous talent. If it's more important for him to protect his glass heart than to follow it. Not that he'd ever make that decision, and I sure as hell wouldn't suggest it. He's got basketballs for eyes. He's married to the game. And provided he can gird himself, he'll do whatever he wants. He'll do marvellous things with a basketball in arenas in Chicago, Los Angeles, New York, Miami. On a billion HD television screens. At the Olympics. This kid has talent we sometimes describe as *generational*. As in *once-in-a-*. If he can find a way to steel himself, if he can graft in that toughness, he'll do it all.

Picking a school is the first step. He must walk right between the crooked teeth of the rabid beast that is the spirit animal of college athletics. He'll entertain me and fifty other recruiters, hear from alumni and boosters, be offered the sun, the moon, and the stars, the plushest campus jobs—as pretext for payments, he could stand next to a program stand at football games, or show up for an hour a week at the campus bookstore—and then he'll choose. With heavy input from Mom, Dad, and, unless I miss my guess, Monique. He'll choose, and commit, and there will be fanfare surrounding that, and more hoopla the day he shows up on campus, and at his first practice.

And so will begin the process, the one that will see him become dried and cured and hardened to it all. He'll let that happen or he'll fail. And this kid can't fail. It can't be allowed to happen. He's got to be ours.

Monique won't last. I know this, but I can't tell him. He has to believe what they have to be invincible and true or he won't commit to us. I see that. He'll stay closer to home—Penn being the natural choice—because he's that beautiful and foolish. A sweet fool. Another reason I love him.

They come to us as good kids, for the most part, and when they leave they're probably still good people, but they've lost something. Or been given too much of something corrupting, perhaps, some uneven regard for what they do. They are told too much that they are better than other people. The best among them refuse to believe it.

I watch the rest of the day's first game and most of the second, which again features two teams that aren't Harrisburg. There are no Division I talents on display, just a court full of boys doing their best. The thought that someone might put in so much work simply to play without an expectation that it will lead them anywhere in life fills me with something like hope. It's probably got to do with the way I felt when I played: never under the impression I'd ever be paid money to do it. For me, as it is for 99.9 percent of those who play, it was a game, and not a pursuit. They, like me, will never be approached by representatives of Duke, or Kansas, or anywhere else. They are free to play and try and sweat and fail, and to have those glorious failures forgotten by the larger world, or simply never seen at all.

But Robert Grainge, and select others like him, are never afforded that luxury, or not for long. They've been tabbed as talents from an early age, been told to concentrate on that one thing, drilled, coached, trained. Eaten, slept, breathed that one thing. Gone to bed in their shorts, worn tournament T-shirts everywhere, gone through a hundred pairs of court shoes. They're the ones whose fathers and mothers we attempt to befriend, or at least whose trust we work to inspire. There's no way around it: in most cases, you have to have their folks on board—the schoolteachers, custodians, bus drivers, cabbies, waiters, cooks, front desk employees, deliverymen, dishwashers, clerks, product testers, assembly-line workers—or you won't get the player. Often as not I'm dealing with just a mom, Dad having exited the picture years earlier, but when you're dealing with both you have to have agreement.

I don't know if I'll get that here. Claudette is warm, a kind, outgoing woman who's clearly proud of her son and all he has done and will do. The attention of me and my ilk is for her validation for all the hours, all the effort, all the sacrifice. She's been only too happy, as a result, to open up. I have been hugged by Claudette Grainge. I have laughed with her. I have eaten her carrot muffins.

Marvin, by comparison, has treated me from the start like someone out to swindle him in a very bad real estate deal. His suspicion is in some way warranted, given that we recruiters are agents of the organizations that seek to take his boy away from home for the first time, to replace his parents as the primary influence in his life. What father wouldn't chafe at that? But most fathers I deal with are also giddy at the prospect of all that awaits their boys. There's usually a point in the courtship process at which I feel I've won Dad over, praised him enough for the way he's raised his son from boy to fine young man, presented him with a rich enough vision of what awaits not just the player but his whole family, and our interaction then passes from standoffish to cordial. Even if they don't choose us, I never walk away feeling I've done anything to upset anyone. I don't make enemies.

Something's different with Marvin, though. It's true enough that some people are suspicious by nature, and that might explain it, but there's an edge to the way he talks to me—or refuses to talk to me—that feels personal. What I don't know is whether he approaches all recruiters the same way, or if this is for me alone. Does he have a warm relationship with Bill from Duke? I've never seen him interact with any of the others enough to know either way. But Monique's mention of Bill leads me to believe that, despite his telling me he had ruled them out, Robert is not so dead set against being a Duke Blue Devil after all.

Marvin has been reserved from our very first point of contact. It's possible, I suppose, that he is slow to let anyone in—he seems to be a patient man—but I suspect otherwise. I suspect, and fear, that I'm not Marvin's pick, and I'm being cut out.

Sometimes I need to remind myself that I have filled my assay bag with some rare minerals in the twenty-one years I've been doing this. I have recruited a third of a national championship team. I have recruited an eventual first overall pick, and six top tens. I have a commendable track record.

And yet my years of experience cannot help me predict

which way Grainge will go, and it fills me with unease. It curdles the cream in my coffee to have come this far into the process and not have a read on things. It gives me honest-to-God pain to think that Bill might really be in the running, might even be out in front of this race.

Fucking Duke.

When the Cougars again take the floor on Saturday evening, against Freire, a charter school team from Philadelphia, they jump out early and never look back. Up twenty-one at the half, Coach Sykes elects to sit Grainge for the second. Groans rise up from the bleachers when play resumes and Robert remains in his warm-ups on the bench, but I can't fault Sykes. They'll win this game easily and earn a spot in Sunday's tournament final. There's no sense risking anything where Grainge is concerned. He's got his future to consider. It's just smart basketball.

I like Sykes. I like what he does with his boys. I like the way his team plays. It doesn't differ too much from our own system. We're known for a style of play that is tough, selfless, contained. Ruthless clampdown defence. There are occasions, admittedly, when our boys sparkle with something showier, a kind of ABA razzle, but usually only once that menacing defence has put the game out of reach. Our entire conference, in fact, is anathema to showboating. Duke, meanwhile, hails from a conference typically more amenable to speed, flash, highlight-ready dunks.

But Sykes is like us. He sees the game as a series of tasks, a set of goals to be attained no matter the score. Grainge is the product of that; the complete embodiment of it, really. I'll say it again: it makes him perfect for us, and us perfect for him.

This has become my mantra. I've said it to Coach B, who needed no convincing. I've said it to the AD. I've said it to the endlessly patient Pam, in a performance that was half thinking aloud, half rehearsal. I've said it to Robert. I've said it to Marvin. I've said it until I was blue in the face. I'd be willing to say it more, to anybody who'd listen, but Marvin Grainge, I know, doesn't want to hear it. And he may be the only person involved I've yet to convince.

I chew on this while I sit over a late night plate of spaghetti and meatballs at the Denny's just off the expressway. Then it's back to the Comfort for a fitful night, bad dreams of Grainge in blue instead of orange, and Pam falling ill with something mysterious. It is not a good night.

What I hope to see when I crack the thick, hotel-grade curtains early on Sunday morning: a fresh blanket of white glistening under a bright winter sun. What I get instead: rain, turning the ground to slush, slicking the streets, making a mess of everything.

I get up slowly, shower, dress, make my way out into the slop. I find a Starbucks, nab a corner table, and with a stack of newspapers, a coffee, and a giant muffin, I try to kill an hour. The consolation game is at two this afternoon, and my plans before then are blessedly few. I'll find a bookstore. Maybe I'll find a museum. I'll have a long lunch. I'll fire off an amorous email to Pam. I'll ignore emails from upstate. If the weather weren't so cold and greasy I might just walk around, discover Harrisburg a little bit. But I've got no interest in that today, not in this mess.

Christmas decorations linger. Cheerily inclusive HAPPY HOLIDAYS signs hang on tenaciously in the bad wind. A dingy HAPPY NEW YEAR banner flaps over the street, lamppost to lamppost. Folks entering the Starbucks stamp their feet and shiver, shake water from their heads. Folks leaving pause to turn up collars, unfold umbrellas. It's what my mother would call "raw" out there.

I must not be far from the Hilton, because as I gaze out the windows who should walk by but Bill, head bowed, cigarette a-dangle, talking to another man I don't recognize but whose brushcut and clothing mark him as one of us. His jacket is red. Indiana, possibly. I hear they've been using somebody new. There are still other suitors, after all. Bill doesn't see me, and for that I'm grateful. It wouldn't be the end of the world if I make it through today's games and maybe one more conversation with Robert or Marvin or both without having to swap barbs with Bill again. I'd be happiest if the next I hear from him is a begrudgingly congratulatory email.

I hold my newspaper up in front of my face, Clouseau-style, in case he doubles back, or suddenly decides he needs himself a grande dark roast.

By the time the consolation game tips off, Bill is in the front row, chatting, backslapping, guffawing. I'm halfway up the bleachers, down near the baseline and safely out of view. The also-rans, those Lions from Altoona and a team from New Jersey called the Bears, sprint and dribble up and down the floor, call out and shoot and clap. The buzzer sounds intermittently. Boys enter the game, other boys leave it. They sit leaning forward, their long arms folded over their knees. They are all limbs, these boys. These boys who will never play Division I ball, let alone pro.

Some of the Harrisburg players are milling around in a tight group down behind the near basket, some in warm-ups, some in street clothes, some in jackets with a menacing cougar spread shoulder blade to shoulder blade. All have headphones strung around their necks and cords snaking down to unseen devices tucked into deep pockets. They are slouchy and lackadaisical, conserving themselves. One feigns a punch at another; they laugh. They have a confident air. Robert is not among them.

Near the end of the third quarter he arrives. I actually see it while I am watching Bill from my spot. Bill's head is scanning, and then it snaps, becomes attentive. I follow his gaze to the doors, and there is Robert, trailed by Claudette and Marvin. Robert, in sweats and with a gym bag slung over his shoulder, looks around, waves to teammates, takes in the score, then hugs his mother. He disappears inside the doors leading to the change rooms, tucking white earphones into his head as he backs through them. He ducks; the learned behaviour of the tall.

My scalp tightens. During the short break between quarters the PA system plays music, a thudding, indistinguishable mass of sound that seems physically threatening. The hair on my neck stands up. I peek over the sea of bobbing heads and I see Bill down there, his usually hunched back suddenly ramrod straight, hands on his knees. His gaze is fixed on those doors that just swallowed Robert. He almost appears hurt.

We're pitching the woo here, hoping for the attentions of a young beau. It's no different from that. I hope Robert will like me and all I represent better than he does Bill. Rejection threatens. That's the basic truth of it.

Just before the buzzer signals the start of the fourth, Bill stands and makes a beeline for the gym's main doors, pulling his phone from a coat pocket on the way. A moment later I see Marvin Grainge head out those same doors.

Things are afoot.

The warm-ups start a half hour before tip-off of the championship game. The Cougars and their opponents, Akron's St. Vincent-St. Mary, form neat lay-up lines, tight and geometrical. Marvin Grainge has returned to the gym and found a seat with Claudette, and Bill is back in his front row perch. Robert appears to be moving at half-speed during warmups, lugubrious and held back. I wonder for a moment if the weekend's schedule has caught up with him.

But once the game tips off I see there's no cause for alarm. Robert is a flurry. Every so often a player seems to dedicate a certain game to the perfection of a specific skill. By midway through the first quarter Robert has eight rebounds. No one beats him to a single ball. He appears light and springy, chasing balls into the air, meeting them exactly where he should. His feet hover over the polished wood floor, his elbows crook to protect his hard-won trophy. Then he stands, swivels his head, and fires off perfect passes to streaking teammates. The Cougars score half their points in transition, sparked by such plays.

The buzzer sounds to end the first quarter. Harrisburg holds a six-point lead on St. Vincent-St. Mary. The game has been fast and entertaining so far, a well-played game of basketball. It has been beautiful to watch, and it has me experiencing that bubbly feeling again.

Mr. and Mrs. Grainge have landed in a pair of folding chairs down near the baseline. From time to time I glance over at them to see what they're up to. When the quarter ends Marvin pats Claudette on the knee, says something to her, and stands to make for the doors. A bathroom break, I'd bet.

My effervescence seizes me, and I rise quickly, clomp

down the metal bleacher steps, and follow Marvin out the doors. I see his greying head moving away from me down a corridor and into the boys' room.

I decide to wait, though it strikes me as a strange thing to do. But strange things are what's called for in this strange business, so when Marvin returns a moment later, wiping his hands on the thighs of his dark pants, I'm leaning against the opposite wall, arms folded.

"Mr. Grainge," I call. "Mr. Grainge!" He looks up, eyes me, and waves his hand in the air, swatting me away like a fly. But I pursue.

Turning his back, he says, "Mr. Eddie, there's nothing to say. We know what you have to offer and Robert will make his decision as he sees fit. You're wasting your time. And mine."

"Mr. Grainge," I say, "I don't want to talk about that. I'm not giving you the sell. I'm not pitching today. I just want to ask you —"

"Ask me what?" he says, and wheels back toward me. His body language says he's standing his ground.

"Mr. Grainge. I just wanted to know if I've done anything to offend you. You just seem, I don't know, put off by me. I wondered if that was something I'd caused."

"Mr. Eddie," he says, then sighs, puts a hand to the back of his neck. "Well, alright, yes. You once said something that didn't sit with me."

"What did I say, Mr. Grainge?"

He exhales, looks into the middle distance over my right shoulder. "You once said a disparaging thing about my profession."

"About bus drivers?"

"That's right. You told Robert that driving a bus was a lousy job that he was lucky he'd never have to do."

At this I give him a relieved smile, one meant to say, "Is that all?" I turn my palms upward and out comes this: "Mr. Grainge, I apologize if anything I said was misconstrued, I honestly do. But the truth is I couldn't have any more respect for what you do."

"It certainly didn't sound that way."

"Mr. Grainge, my father drove a bus for eighteen years," I say, and it's nearly true. "Cincinnati. ATU Local 627."

At this, Marvin Grainge, the toughest nut I have ever had to crack, straightens his shoulders and stands a little taller. His face softens into something very like a smile.

"That so," he says. "Well, Mr. Eddie, I'm afraid I had you wrong."

"I'm glad to hear that, Mr. Grainge," I say.

"Yes," Marvin says, then makes as though to say something further, but stops himself.

"Okay," I say, and the short buzzer sounds, calling the players back to the floor for the second quarter. It is muffled through the gym's heavy doors, but we both hear it, and take it as our signal to head back inside. I hold my arm out indicating Marvin should go first, and he does the same to me. A ref's whistle blows. We chuckle, then Marvin relents, hurries ahead of me.

As we walk toward the doors and the charged artificial light beyond, a gasp goes up from all those assembled. We can hear it through the doors. It's theatrical in quality, a remarkable sound, and in its wake the very air has changed.

We both quicken, rushing inside, and see people converging all at once, as though the gym's floor has folded in on itself. The area beneath the near basket is dense with humanity. Sykes is lying on his stomach next to Robert, who is on his back, clutching his left knee with one arm, the other slung over his anguished face. Marvin races through the crowd and out onto the court, and is immediately kneeling over his son. The Cougars' manager, a young man with an overstuffed fanny pack, is crouched over Robert, his hands hovering over the knee in a shamanistic pose, but seemingly unable to touch it. Robert writhes.

People still in the bleachers stand with their hands atop their heads, or held to their faces. No one speaks. I am standing with my hands on my hips, wondering what's left to see, when Bill shuffles past me and makes his way from the gym and out, out into the sleet-filled night. Headed, I can only assume, out of Harrisburg altogether, and back to North Carolina.

After a moment I too turn to leave. There is really nothing left to see. In my heart I know that. The early dark has fallen on Harrisburg, and the roads will be awful. I don't look forward to what lies ahead, but it can't be avoided. I turn to make for my car, for the dark and slick road. I'm already on my way back upstate, back to Pam, back to my home. Other young men in other gyms demand my attention now. In the morning I'll start to put the press on the next names on our list. I just hope we aren't too far behind on them now. We have holes that need to be filled.

FAT ALBERT

What had happened was that I had assembled a thermonuclear device in the garage, more or less accidentally. I guess I had some idea what I was doing, but I didn't have a set plan, per se. It was just, what if I put this here? There were some instructions downloaded from the Internet, sure, and some books checked out of the library, but it wasn't my intent to have it become a big deal. I certainly didn't have a List of Demands, like they kept asking me.

I had several main concerns while it was all going on, but the biggest one had to do with the damage their Mobile Command Centre—essentially a tricked-out RV—had done to my lawn when they rolled up. I was thinking about the levelling and reseeding I was going to have to do.

It was embarrassing, too, I have to say. It felt like an unwarranted level of scrutiny. They'd managed to evacuate the neighbourhood, but not before that awkward half hour or so when all the neighbours were standing around in a tight arc that cut across the street, which I guess they'd closed, and onto the sidewalk out front of Jerry's house. There was a whole lot of milling about and, I don't have to guess, gossip taking place. They were probably saying this had to do with my being laid off, but it truly didn't. Springer Electric had dumped a nice severance in my lap, and I was kind of enjoying my time off. It gave me time to putter, fix a few things that had been bothering me, to reorganize the tool room and, you know, to build the device, which I had nicknamed Fat Albert for the sake of avoiding clunky monikers like "The Device."

My only motivation, if I even had one, was to prove to myself that it could be done with simple household materials and a well-stocked toolbox. And guess what?

When I realized that I'd done it, I began to think that I ought to write it down somewhere so I didn't forget how I'd managed to do it. Then I thought, you know, this might be useful to others, or at least impressive. I thought maybe I would start a blog.

There was no cause. No Cause. No political statement, save my belief in self-reliance, a can-do DIY streak that usually looks like changing your own oil, performing your own renovations with or without the prescribed permits, and not expecting government handouts to see you through life's rough patches. That, and the feeling that what happens in my garage is really only my business and nobody else's.

The joke is that one stray comment to the mailman was all that was required to let the world in on my secret. I was working one warm spring morning with the garage door up, just putting some finishing touches on Fat Albert, a bit of paint mostly, and he came by with a handful of junk mail. He doesn't usually say much, just a curt hello, but he saw the box and wires, and he stood puzzled for a moment, that floppy hat on his head, his twin saddlebags by his sides, bulging with envelopes and flyers, and he said, "What on earth is that?"

And I, feeling prideful, had to boast, "It's a bomb. A nuclear device. Crazy, right? I just figured I'd give it a shot. Just a thing to see if I could do it."

"Come on," he said.

"Seriously," I said.

"Jesus."

"Yeah. A thermonuclear bomb."

"Really?" he said. "Like, really?"

"It was pretty easy, actually. You could do it yourself, I'd bet. With stuff you have lying around the house, like old smoke detectors, and a couple of hours on Wikipedia."

"Right," he said, and he laughed a kind of thin, nervous laugh.

"I mean it," I said, but he was already halfway across the lawn to Mrs. Gale's house and, I'd bet, by the time he reached the corner, by the time he figured he was out of earshot, he was digging his phone out of his pocket and notifying the relevant authorities.

At that same moment, here's what I was thinking: it's the kind of thing he'll laugh about later.

But soon all hell broke loose. And while I sat in the garage trying to convince the negotiator that I wasn't going to send us all to meet our maker and that my only demand was that I not be shot when I left the garage, I got to thinking that Carolyn, my ex, would have a field day with this once she heard.

With all that time just to sit and think, I also found my mind settling on good times, on the absolute nuke she'd been, once upon a time. About how explosive we were together, and how that was a way I knew I'd never feel again. The red-and-blue strobe was what did it, the silent flashing of the lights on those emergency vehicles, the cruisers and SUVs parked out there on my bluegrass and creeping thyme. I closed my eyes and was reminded of camera flashes, Greek discos, fireworks displays, sparklers atop her twenty-fifth birthday cake. I got wistful.

Once, in Mexico, I pulled a burning Roman candle from her long auburn hair. She was twenty-four and had the power to stop my heart. There was a brass band standing atop a wall. The wall surrounded a house that had never been built. They were playing fast and loud, wearing matching purple suits. All of the lean, pouty boys of the town of San Juan Cosala were carrying small fireworks in their pockets. The would take them out, and four or five of the boys would huddle around one cigarette lighter or book of matches, and once the fuses were lit they would run shrieking in every direction until theirs went off. We were in a procession of people—townspeople, visitors— and we had no idea what was happening. We were being herded down narrow, uneven streets. Above us effigies and Catherine wheels hung on wires. Carolyn laughed the whole time. There came a whistling noise that grew terrible and big in my ears, and all of a sudden, while she was still laughing, a ball of fire settled in her hair, just near her right shoulder. We were beneath the band then, loud *oompah-oompahs* thudding in our ears, and she didn't hear me shout, "Your hair!" I just reached in and grabbed it, flung it to the ground, and stomped on it.

"Wow!" she cried. Our noses were stuffed with the smells of sulphur, liquor, the jacaranda trees. Our hearts were crammed with too much regard for money, for ourselves, and for our own love, which we believed to be made of carelessness and hope, all of which would come to play hands in our eventual dissolution. But not yet, no no. The truth is that our erroneous beliefs would sustain us for several years yet.

And in the bright, fresh morning we found her singed hairs. She brushed them painfully out, our ears still ringing with music and explosions.

In Athens, a couple of years earlier, there were riot police for something we didn't understand, and we watched the armoured men move a crowd back a city block while the flashing lights bounced off the empty, unfinished highrise across from our third-floor room. We had been on the balcony, but she said she thought she saw someone preparing a Molotov cocktail, and so we moved inside. She was two months out of Queen's with her masters degree, staring at a lifetime of student debt, but she said we had to go to Greece, and so we went. This was our first night in Athens, and we were pinned in our tiny hotel room by whatever was happening in the street below us.

When finally we grew bored of watching we pulled the drapes, finished a bottle of retsina, and then made love. This we did with the intensity of a street battle. She said, "Don't you ever try to get away from me." The noise outside was like a physical thing inside of which we had become lost, consumed. I thought for a moment that we were in the middle of the riot, that the windows had fallen away or the door had been blown off its hinges; there were voices that sounded like they were next to us in that room, standing over us. That anticipation of a club coming down onto my head heightened everything. We deserved to be arrested, detained. There were violations of decency, decorum. It was uncivil.

Afterwards the flashing lights were still coming through and around the thin brown curtains. Carolyn sat at the end of the bed with her legs drawn up to her chest. The lights made her red hair even redder. I said, "I love the colour of your hair."

She said, "You've never seen my real hair colour."

In the morning, in the dingy restaurant on the second floor, over bitter coffee, we asked the waiter what the excitement had been.

"I don't know of anything," he said.

"Outside? Last night?"

"Oh, yes," he said, and then explained that young people were upset over a plan to close the nightclubs of Athens earlier, at 4:00 instead of 5:00 in the morning, I think he said.

"They riot for that?" Carolyn asked.

"Oh, for anything," the waiter answered.

And yes, sure, while I'm picking scabs here, there was my father. The flashing lights on the lawn of my parents' house, my house, when I was nine years old. They lit up my mother's face and her long brown hair. I saw grey where I had never noticed it before, at her temples and forehead, and I wondered if it had just appeared there, that evening, in the time between when she and I had returned from visiting Mrs. Curtis down the block, and I had heard the car running and opened the door into the garage and seen Dad there, the driver's seat tilted back, his face waxen and blank, and when they had loaded him into the ambulance and driven him away. It was the seventeenth of April. There was a mist in the air, the grass was wet, the air smelled like mud. After the ambulance left the police car remained, its lights still bouncing off the shining lawn and the slick pavement, the house's aluminum siding. I left my mother's side for a moment and walked, in a daze, toward the house. I don't think I had yet taken in what I had seen, I hadn't made sense of it, that he had meant to do that, meant for us to find him. That he had been waiting until we were gone. I sleepwalked around the side of the house, slowly, dumbly, and saw there the garden shed that he and I had begun building the previous autumn, started and not finished, a frame without walls or roof, appearing ghostlike in the stray arms of the flashing blue-and-red light.

I turned again and looked across the street, at the houses there, and the great, dark forest behind them. That was the end of the known world. I had thought that the night we moved into that house, when I was six. That night, I remember very clearly thinking that none of the world was known to me, and that it might never be.

They took us in a police car, its lights no longer flashing, to the hospital to confirm what we both knew, mother and her only child. She did not speak, not a word. They towed away the car, a white Ford Pinto. Mom sold the house, and we moved into a townhouse in another neighbourhood. She cut her hair short and wore it that way for the rest of her life. It seems to me that she wore that same expression, too, the uncomprehending one she'd had on the front lawn, in the damp, electric air, maybe staring across at that same forest, until she died last year. My poor mother.

And let's not forget Springer Electric, where I'd put in fifteen years, me sitting in my little cube there, and the red light on my office phone that flashed for an incoming call. It was a Monday morning, and the layoff rumours were flying fast. And then it started, 9:00 AM sharp. By 9:30 everyone knew what was happening, that Deb, the HR woman, was calling people into her office to give them the news one at a time. So we all just sat dumbly by our phones, waiting, we hoped, for nothing. All morning. You'd hear the phone ring a cubicle over, or down the hall, and your heart would catch in your throat. At a quarter after eleven my red light began blinking, the quiet, synthesized *bloop-bloop* of the ringtone. In the moment I thought that maybe it was someone else, but the call display window said INT-OFFICE: HR.

That was eight months ago, and I was already hurting thanks to the payments to Carolyn. But the severance helped things, really. Put me on a different course, gave me reason to think that I'd find myself in a new life that fit me better than the old one. I got to read a stack of books I'd been meaning to get to, I got to finish some projects. I woke those mornings after the layoff marinating in the belief that the world rewards a patient man.

All of these things make quite a list, I agree. Divorce, job loss, the death of my father. Add it all up, right? It's all there. Well, whatever. Who hasn't suffered traumas? Who's coasting through this life unscathed?

This is what I said over the phone to the negotiator after he brought up these well-researched facts about my life. "We know what you've gone through," he said, "with your marital troubles, losing your job, the way your father died…" Probably they'd been talking to Carolyn.

"This isn't about that," I said. "Any of that. This isn't about anything. It's just a thing I did."

"Of course, Mr. Wardell," he said. "I understand, Matthew. Can I call you Matthew?"

"I'd prefer not."

"Of course." He was trying very hard not to upset me, which I found kind of funny. I figured, in a town like Cavanagh, Ontario, he probably didn't have a lot of opportunity to use his negotiator skills. He was probably just a guy, a cop, who got roped into a two-day seminar or something, just got the qualification, and here he was. That made me laugh. But it didn't make me like him, and it didn't change the fact that here I was, penned in my own garage with a marvellous bit of work that should've earned me an entirely different sort of attention. Look at this, I wanted to shout, I did this myself! How great is that?

I hadn't calculated megatonnage or anything like that, but I'm pretty sure Fat Albert would have rendered most, if not all, of this town uninhabitable for the foreseeable future. It'd be marked on maps as CAVANAGH EXCLU-SION ZONE, or something like that. You'd have to sign your life away to walk down my street in a radiation suit.

In the end, at about three or four in the morning, I took the negotiator's assurances that the tactical guys weren't going to shoot me or grind my head into the driveway if I came out, and I just pushed the button for the opener and waited for the big door to go up. The flashing lights filled the whole space then, the red-and-blue light dancing on everything: on the lawnmower, on the cases of empties, on the mountain bike I'd bought last year and hadn't really used. It danced on the birdhouse I'd begun the week before.

Their bomb guys—I think they had to come in from Toronto—got a pretty big kick out of Fat Albert. "He could have done it," they said, which added to the charges, actually. If it had been a hoax, if Albert had been an empty box with a few wires sticking out, a prop, then at worst I'd have been looking at mischief.

There's a chance I've overstated how easy it was. My electrical engineering degree certainly helped, and it didn't hurt to have had access to certain materials when I was still at Springer. But I'm still kind of in awe over how easy it was.

Why, why, why, they wanted to know. I kept trying to impress upon them that it wasn't some great design, it wasn't pushed along by belief, or zealotry, or anger. "I just like projects," I said.

"You weren't really going to press that button, were you?" one young guy wearing his dad's suit asked me. I waved my hand dismissively.

What I didn't tell him, of course, and what I'm not telling you, is that I not only thought about pressing the button, but I went ahead and did it. A couple of hours before I walked out of the garage. I was so tired, you know. I closed my eyes and squeezed the big, red trigger. I wanted to know what it would be like at the centre of that enormous flash. But nothing happened. Something in the wiring, I guess, some small thing, a screw I hadn't sufficiently tightened. It left me with such a deflated feeling, to be honest. Like, oh, hey, great, here's the rest of my life and it's all still laid out in front of me. All the broken things. All the missing parts.

ACKNOWLEDGEMENTS

Sincere thanks to the crew at Invisible—Robbie, Megan, Leigh, and Nic—for believing in this book.

Many of these stories, in their initial forms, needed to be beaten into shape, or stripped down and rebuilt altogether. I'm grateful to my editor, Michelle Sterling, for her keen eye and her patience.

For publishing earlier versions of several of these stories, and for the guidance and input of their editors, I'm grateful to the following publications: *Little Fiction*, *PRISM international*, *The Puritan*, *Hobart*, *This Magazine*, *The New Quarterly*, *Scrivener Creative Review*, *Found Press*.

To the readers—Rick Taylor, Eric Fershtman, and others—who've offered me their eyes and their suggestions, I say thank you.

And lastly, thanks are due to my family, for their unending support and understanding.

"Well, it's better, anyway."

INVISIBLE PUBLISHING is a not-for-profit publishing company that produces contemporary works of fiction, creative non-fiction, and poetry. We publish material that's engaging, literary, current, and uniquely Canadian. We're small in scale, but we take our work, and our mission, seriously. We produce culturally relevant titles that are well written, beautifully designed, and affordable.

Invisible Publishing has been in operation for just over half a decade. Since releasing our first fiction titles in the spring of 2007, our catalogue has come to include works of graphic fiction and non-fiction, pop culture biographies, experimental poetry and prose.

Invisible Publishing continues to produce high quality literary works, we're also home to the Bibliophonic series and the Snare imprint.

If you'd like to know more please get in touch.
info@invisiblepublishing.com

Invisible Publishing
Halifax & Toronto